Back by Popular Demand

A collector's edition of favorite titles
from one of the world's best-loved
romance authors. Harlequin is proud to
bring back these sought after titles and
present them as one cherished collection.

BETTY NEELS:
COLLECTOR'S EDITION

A GEM OF A GIRL
WISH WITH THE CANDLES
COBWEB MORNING
HENRIETTA'S OWN CASTLE
CASSANDRA BY CHANCE
VICTORY FOR VICTORIA
SISTER PETERS IN AMSTERDAM
THE MAGIC OF LIVING
SATURDAY'S CHILD
FATE IS REMARKABLE
A STAR LOOKS DOWN
HEAVEN IS GENTLE

HARLEQUIN®

Betty Neels spent her childhood and youth in Devonshire before training as a nurse and midwife. She was an army nursing sister during the war, married a Dutchman, and subsequently lived in Holland for fourteen years. She now lives with her husband in Dorset, and has a daughter and grandson. Her hobbies are reading, animals, old buildings and, of course, writing. Betty started to write on retirement from nursing, incited by a lady in a library bemoaning the lack of romantic novels.

Mrs. Neels is always delighted to receive fan letters, but would truly appreciate it if they could be directed to Harlequin Mills & Boon Ltd., 18-24 Paradise Road, Richmond, Surrey, TW9 1SR, England.

Books by Betty Neels

BETTY NEELS

VICTORY FOR VICTORIA

COLLECTOR'S EDITION

HARLEQUIN®

TORONTO • NEW YORK • LONDON
AMSTERDAM • PARIS • SYDNEY • HAMBURG
STOCKHOLM • ATHENS • TOKYO • MILAN • MADRID
PRAGUE • WARSAW • BUDAPEST • AUCKLAND

ISBN 0-373-83391-1

VICTORY FOR VICTORIA

First North American Publication 1998.

Copyright © 1972 by Betty Neels.

CHAPTER ONE

IT was going to rain very shortly; the grey woolly clouds, blown into an untidy heap by the wind, were tearing across the sky, half hiding the distant island of Sark and turning the water to a reflected darkness. Miss Victoria Parsons, making her brisk way along the cliff path from St Peter Port to Fermain Bay, paused to watch them, sighing with content and pleasure as she did so, for it was the first day of her holiday and she was free to tramp where she wished, uncaring of wind and rain, uncaring too of her appearance, a fact amply demonstrated by her attire; a guernsey, quite two sizes too large for her, which gave her slim curves a deceiving bulkiness, and a pair of slacks, well fitting but decidedly worn, but after several months of nurse's uniform they were a delight to wear besides, there was no one to see her on this windy March afternoon. She stood, sniffing the air and calculating how long it would be before the clouds reached Guernsey and the rain started. Ten minutes, she thought, perhaps a little less, and she was barely halfway. She had passed the new houses built overlooking the sea, there was nothing now until she reached Fermain Bay, only the narrow up and down, roundabout path between the trees, halfway between the cliff top and the sea below. She went a little nearer the edge of the cliff now and stared down at the rocks below and a gust of wind tore at her hair, loosening the pins, so that she took the remainder out and let the coppery mass tangle in the wind.

A drop of rain fell on to her face as she turned back

on to the path once more and she remembered, just in time, the old disused powder magazine cut into the cliff, not so very far away. She could shelter there; the rain was coming down in earnest now and while her guernsey kept her dry, her hair was already hanging wetly around her shoulders and the rain pouring down her face, and by the time she reached the magazine she was drenched and a little breathless from hurrying.

The magazine was built of granite and had lost its door long ago, but its four walls were solid, as was its roof. She squelched inside; here at least it was dry—the rain wouldn't last long and there was time enough before she need be home again. It was dim inside and quite warm, she turned her back on the interior to peer out at the sky, squeezing the wet from her sopping hair as she did so; it might be an idea to take off her guernsey and give it a good shake— She was on the point of pulling it over her head when a voice from the furthest corner of the magazine said mildly: 'Er—if you would wait one moment...'

Victoria spun round, indignation at being frightened out of her wits eclipsing her fear. She snapped: 'Who are you, and what are you doing here?'

'Why, as to who I am, I imagine that's hardly relevant to the occasion, and I'm doing exactly the same as you— sheltering from the weather.'

The owner of the voice had advanced towards her as he spoke—a tall man, wide in the shoulder, with dark hair and blue eyes and the kind of good looks which on any other occasion would have caused her to wish to know him better. But not now; she said crossly: 'You could have said something...'

'My dear good woman, I was sitting in the furthest corner of this—er—building with my eyes closed.' He eyed her coolly. 'Having a nice rest,' he added. 'You disturbed it.' And while she was still searching indignantly for a rejoinder to this candid remark, he went on: 'You're very wet. Here, have my handkerchief and at least wipe your face.'

His look implied that her appearance was so awful that drying her face wouldn't be of much use anyway. She took the handkerchief he was holding out to her, dried her face and began on her hair; it was a pity that her usually ready tongue was incapable of fashioning any of the biting remarks jostling each other so hopelessly inside her pretty head. She seethed quietly, handed the handkerchief back with a muttered thank you and retreated against a wall.

'Now don't do that,' said her companion in a matter-of-fact voice. 'Come here and I'll dry as much of your hair as I can.' And when she hesitated, 'Don't be a fool, girl,' he added in a lazily amused voice which sent the blood to her cheeks. It would be silly to refuse and anyway she liked his face—his mouth was firm and kind and his eyes steady. She advanced with dignity and turned her back at his bidding while he began to rub her hair with the damp handkerchief.

'Untamed,' he remarked, 'your hair, I mean. Don't you find it a nuisance?'

Really, thought Victoria, what a man he was! Could he say nothing pleasant? He had done nothing but find fault with her, and now her hair... Her beautiful tawny eyes flashed, she said with deceptive sweetness: 'No, not in the least—I like it like this,' and heard him laugh softly.

'Ah,' he commented in the same mild voice with which he had first spoken, 'one of those young women who are above fashion and suchlike nonsense. There, that is the best I can do, and the rain has stopped.' He stuffed the sopping handkerchief into his pocket. 'Shall we go? You're on your way back to St Peter Port, I suppose?'

Victoria gave him a considered glance. She could of course go on to Fermain Bay as she had planned to do, but on the other hand, although he had vexed her quite unnecessarily and frightened her out of her life, she felt a strong urge to find out a little more about her companion. When, after a moment, he said: 'You're quite safe, you know,' any doubts about the advisability of joining him on the return walk were instantly swamped by indignation, and as if that wasn't enough he added: 'It's rather a lonely walk for a girl on her own, isn't it?'

Victoria looked down her nicely shaped nose. 'I'm twenty-three,' she informed him in a voice which, though controlled, throbbed with anger.

'That isn't quite what I meant.' He spoke carelessly as he turned away from her. 'The path will be abominably muddy. Shall I go first?'

She walked behind him, answering his occasional remarks with a politeness which admitted of no wish to be friendly on her part. Not that this seemed to worry him; his own friendliness was quite unforced and he made no attempt to find out anything about her, and Victoria, who was used to men looking at her at least twice and certainly wanting to know something about her, felt let down. She wasn't a conceited girl, but she was a remarkably pretty one and she would have been a fool not to know it. It irked her now that she had made no impression on this man; he had even implied that she had no idea how to dress. She eyed his broad back resentfully; it was a pity that she was unlikely to meet him again when she was dressed with her usual careful eye to fashion.

'Do you live here?' she asked.

He didn't slow his pace but said over one shoulder,

'No,' and nothing more. She was right, her chance of seeing him again was negligible. For some reason she felt sorry, then she told herself that it was because she had taken a dislike to him and it would have given her great satisfaction to have met him again, herself becomingly dressed, and put him in his place. She began reviewing her wardrobe, deciding what she would wear for that occasion, and then grinned ruefully to herself because of course they wouldn't meet again. He was probably an early visitor to the island; there was nothing about his clothes to suggest otherwise—a guernsey, just like her own—but a great many visitors bought them as a matter of course—and bedford cord slacks which had seen better days. She longed to ask where he came from; she had detected a faint accent when he spoke. Before she could stop herself, she asked: 'You're not English, are you?' and exactly as before, got a 'No' over one shoulder. After that she didn't speak again, not until they were past St George's Fort and the town was in full view, not ten minutes' walk away. He stopped then and asked, 'Which way do you go?'

She answered briefly, 'Havelet,' not caring if he knew where that was or not. Apparently he did, for he said: 'I'm going to the harbour. Would you like me to walk up with you first?'

She forbore to tell him that, born and bred on the island, she knew every yard of it, and as for St Peter Port, she could walk blindfold through its length and breadth and know exactly where she was. Her reply was a sedate refusal. She thought, she added pleasantly, that she could find her way. His, 'Oh, good,' was disconcertingly casual.

They parted at the end of the cliff path, she to turn up the narrow hill away from the sea, he presumably to walk along the sea front to the harbour. The Jersey boat was in, so possibly he was going to board her—a great many people came over for the day, although he didn't look like a day tripper, for despite his clothes he had an air of assurance, almost arrogance. Victoria frowned as she wished him a coolly polite goodbye, and was left gaping at his parting words.

'You'd be quite a pretty girl if you smiled more often,' he pronounced—and he didn't say goodbye either. She crossed the road and then turned to watch him walk away without a backward glance.

Her parents lived almost at the top of Havelet, in a pleasant elderly house tucked away from the road. It had a glorious view of the harbour and the sea beyond, and a garden which, although not large, was a riot of colour for most of the year. Victoria climbed the steep, narrow road without effort, went through the gate—just wide enough to take the car—and into the house through its open front door.

'If that's you, Victoria, shut the door, will you, darling?' called her mother from somewhere upstairs. 'Did you have a nice walk?' her parent continued as she began a descent of the staircase. Victoria shut the door and turned to meet her mother. Mrs Parsons was a large woman, still very handsome and despite her size, surprisingly youthful in appearance. She had a commanding presence and a voice which, while not loud, was so clear that no one ever failed to hear it. She paused on the stairs now and peered down at her daughter.

'Victoria, my dear child, did you really go out looking like that?'

'No,' said Victoria reasonably, 'I was dry then, Mother. I got caught in that downpour.' She advanced to plant an affectionate kiss on her mother's cheek, reaching up to do so because Mrs Parsons was five feet eleven inches tall and Victoria, the eldest of her four daughters, was only five feet six. Her mother returned the salute with warmth.

'Well, I'm sure you enjoyed yourself, child. I must say you need the fresh air after London—why you have to work there...' she sighed. 'Your father could speak to—'

'Yes, Mother dear,' interposed Victoria hastily, 'but I do like nursing, you know, and when the Old Crow retires next year, I'm hoping to get the ward.'

Her mother fingered the sleeve of her guernsey. 'You're wet,' she said rather absently, and then: 'Don't you want to marry and settle down, Vicky dear?'

'Only when I meet the right man, Mother.' She had a peculiarly vivid memory of the man in the powder magazine as she spoke and dismissed it as nonsensical.

'But they fall over each other...'

Her daughter smiled. 'I bet they fell over each other for you before you met Father.'

Mrs Parsons's composed features broke into a smile. 'Yes, they did. Your father will be home in a minute, so you'd better go and change, Vicky—your sisters are upstairs already. They take so long to dress, try and hurry them up, dear.'

Victoria said, 'Yes, Mother,' and went up the stairs to a half landing which had a door on either side of it; she passed these, however, and went through the archway at the back of the landing and up half a dozen more stairs leading to a corridor running at right angles to them.

There was a good deal of noise here; her youngest sister, Stephanie, sixteen years old and already bidding fair to outshine them all with her beauty, was hammering on the bathroom door with a good deal of strength.

'Come out, Louise,' she shouted. 'You've been in there ages, you're mean...' She broke off as she saw

Victoria. 'Vicky darling,' she begged, 'get her out, I'll never be ready...'

Victoria approached the door and knocked gently. 'Louise?' she called persuasively, 'do come and see my dress and tell me what you think of it.'

The door was flung open and her sister sailed out. 'OK,' she said, 'but let it be now, this minute, so that I'm not interrupted while I'm doing my face. Where's Amabel?'

'Here.' Amabel was two years younger than Victoria and the quietest of the four. The two of them followed Victoria to her room and fell on to her bed while she took the dress from her cupboard and held it up for their inspection. It was a midi dress of leaf green crêpe with a demure collar like a pie-frill above a minute bodice and a very full skirt. It was admired and carefully examined and Louise said, 'You'll put us all in the shade, Vicky.'

Victoria shook her head. She was a very pretty girl, but her three sisters took after their mother; they were tall—even Stephanie was five feet ten and she hadn't stopped growing—and magnificently built with glowing blonde hair and blue eyes. Their faces were beautiful. Victoria, putting the dress away again, looked at them and wondered how it was that she, the eldest, should have copper hair and tiger's eyes and be of only a moderate height; she was slim too and although she had a lovely face it couldn't match the beauty of the other three girls. She grinned at them suddenly. 'Me for the next bath—I'll be ten minutes,' and started for the bathroom, shedding the guernsey as she went.

They collected in her room as they were ready, squabbling mildly and criticising each other's dresses as she sat at the dressing table putting up her hair. She had combed it back from her forehead and arranged it in three thick loops on her neck and it had taken a long time, but the result, she considered, staring at her reflection in the mirror, had been worth the effort. Rather different from her hairstyle of that afternoon—it was a pity... She dismissed the thought and said briskly: 'If we're ready we'd better go down.' She eyed her sisters with loving admiration. 'I must say you all look smashing, my dears.' And they did, with their fair hair combed smoothly over their magnificent shoulders and their gay dresses. As usual, they would create a small sensation when they entered the restaurant presently. She smiled proudly at them, for they were such splendid creatures and the dearest sisters.

Their parents were waiting for them downstairs. Victoria's mother, splendid in a violet crêpe dress which was the exact foil to her grey, simply-dressed hair, was sitting by the small fire in the sitting room, and her father was standing at the window, looking out on to the harbour, but he turned round as they went in and crowded around him, for they hadn't seen him since early that morning. He saluted them each in turn with a fatherly kiss and being just a little taller than they were, he was able to look down upon them with benign affection. He said now:

'You all look very nice, I must say. Shall we walk or do you want the car?

A routine question which was merely a concession to their finery, for the hotel was only a few minutes' walk away, but it was asked each time they dined there, and that was frequently, to mark each of their birthdays as well as the first evening of Victoria's holidays. They chorused a happy 'no, thank you', picked up their various coats and wraps and left the house in a cheerful chattering group with Mr and Mrs Parsons leading the way.

The restaurant was full, but they had a table in one of the windows overlooking the harbour. Mrs Parsons, sweeping regally through the doors, acknowledged the head waiter's bow with a gracious smile and sailed in his wake, seemingly oblivious of the four eye-catching girls behind her, and they, by now used to being stared at and not in the least disconcerted by it, followed her; Stephanie first, then Amabel, Louise and lastly Victoria, quite dwarfed by her sisters and her father behind her.

They sat down, with Victoria on her father's left with her back to the semi-circular room, and her parents facing each other at each end of the table. They had finished their soup and were awaiting their crabmeat patties when Stephanie, sitting opposite Victoria, remarked:

'There's a man across the room—I've never seen him before.' A remark sufficient to awaken interest in the two younger Miss Parsons, for they knew most of the young men on the island and they had deduced, quite rightly, that the man was good-looking and tolerably young—otherwise she wouldn't have noticed him.

It was Louise, sitting next to Victoria, who asked: 'How old? Is he nice-looking? Dark or fair?' Before her sister could reply her mother interposed.

'Louise, you should know better, encouraging Stephanie like that! We don't know him, I fancy, do we, dear?' She raised her eyebrows at her husband, who laughed.

'My dear,' he said, 'I can hardly inspect the man without embarrassment on both our parts, but if you've never seen him before, then I'm fairly sure that I haven't either.'

Victoria speared her last morsel of patty. 'All the same, I'm dying of curiosity and I can't turn round, can I?' She looked enquiringly at her mother, who smiled a little and said, 'Oh, very well, but he's with a very pretty young woman, so it really is a waste of Stephanie's time.'

Stephanie ignored the young woman. 'He's very large and he's got dark hair and one of those high foreheads—he doesn't laugh very much, but he looks swoony when he smiles. He's got one of those straight noses, just a little too big for his face, if you know what I mean—he turns me on.'

This vivid description met with her sister's interested approval, but her mother said briskly before any of them could speak:

'That is a vulgar expression which I dislike, Stephanie, you will be good enough to remember that.'

'Amabel says it,' muttered her youngest born rebelliously.

'Amabel is twenty-one,' said her mother sweepingly as she helped herself to poached salmon, and Stephanie made a mutinous face so that Victoria said swiftly, before the mutiny should become an open one:

'I thought of going down to Castle Cornet tomorrow to see Uncle Gardener'—the curator and an old family friend, and such a ferocious horticulturist that they had called him by that name all their lives. 'Anyone want to come with me?'

A cheerful babble of argument broke out as she had known it would. Her holiday this time was a short one, and her family, anxious that she shouldn't waste a precious minute of it, were full of suggestions.

'It'll have to be in the afternoon, then,' said Amabel. 'Remember we're going to the market in the morning and you've got some shopping to do—if you don't do it straight away you're sure to forget it and go back with only half the things you want.'

'There's a dress in the Jaguar shop,' began Louise. They settled down to a happy discussion as to what

Vicky should do with her days and the stranger across the restaurant was forgotten—or almost. Only Stephanie glanced across at him once or twice and Victoria, eating her ice pudding with a healthy appetite, wondered if he could possibly be the man she had met that afternoon. It seemed so unlikely that she dismissed the idea from her mind and bent it instead to the conversation going on around her.

They lingered over the cheese board and the coffee; it was only when Mr Parsons suggested that they should go to the bar below the restaurant for a drink before they returned home that the family made a move. They left as they had entered, Mrs Parsons in the lead, her daughters following and Mr Parsons ambling along behind them, and this time the girls contrived to get a good look at the man Stephanie had described. Victoria, waiting for the others to file out ahead of her, had the best chance of all of them to study him. It was the man of the afternoon, this time elegantly dressed and, as her mother had remarked, in the company of a very pretty woman. He was smiling across the table at her and as she lifted her hand for a brief moment Victoria, who had excellent sight, clearly saw the rings on her left hand. His fiancée, his wife even. She felt a sudden surprising sensation of loss and after that one look followed Louise through the restaurant, aware as she went that he had seen her.

She spent the next morning shopping with her sisters, stocking up on soap and lipsticks and face powder because they were all so much cheaper in Guernsey. They were clustered round the door of 'La Parfumerie' arguing where they should go for their coffee when Victoria saw him again, looking exactly as he had done when she had met him, and accompanied by a man of his own age, similarly attired. He was holding a very small boy by the hand too, which substantiated her guess about the pretty girl with the rings. She stared after him and Louise, looking up, caught her at it and said at once: 'There he is again, that man Stephanie was so smitten with—and that was a waste of time, ducky, he's trailing a kid.'

They all laughed, and if Victoria's laughter sounded a little hollow, nobody noticed. They went, arm-in-arm, into the arcade, to Maison Carré for coffee and enormous cream puffs, which should have spoiled their appetites for lunch, but didn't.

As it turned out, Victoria went alone to Castle Cornet, for it began to rain after lunch and none of the others liked the idea of getting wet doing something which they could so easily do on a fine day, but Vicky, they all agreed, should certainly go if she had a mind to. After all, it was her holiday, and she, who would have gone whatever her sisters had said, agreed pleasantly to be home in good time because they were all going to the theatre that evening. All parties being satisfied, she set off, sensibly dressed in slacks and a hooded anorak, down the hill and along the Esplanade, deserted now, and along Castle Pier to the castle. Uncle Gardener would be on the battlements, brooding over his spring flowers whatever the weather.

She entered by the visitors' gateway and waved to the woman sitting idly in the little booth where summer visitors paid their fees, and walked on to the Outer Bailey and so eventually to the ramparts, where sure enough, Uncle Gardener was working. He was at the far end and Victoria made her way unhurriedly towards him, pausing to look down to the rocks below and then out to sea. There was a wind, but it was surprisingly light for the time of year and the sea had been beaten flat by the rain. All the same, it was hardly the weather to take a boat out, she thought, watching a yacht, its white-painted hull and brown sails showing up vividly against the greyness of the sea and sky, coming out of the harbour, running fast before the wind, going south towards Jerbourg Point. She could see the orange-coloured lifejackets of the two people aboard—two men, one at the tiller, the other…there was no reason to be so sure that it was the man she had met on the way to Fermain Bay, only—even at that distance—his size.

Victoria began to run along the path beside the battlements until she reached Uncle Gardener, who looked up and smiled. 'Uncle,' she wasted no time in greeting him, 'have you got your binoculars with you?' and when he handed them to her without speaking, turned and raced back along the ramparts. It was the same man, and his companion was the man she had seen him with that morning. There was no sign of anyone else on board, but they could be in the cabin, for it was a fair-sized boat—a Sea King—built for a family, although surely he wouldn't take his family out on a day such as this one was? She watched it pass the castle and alter course out to sea—Jersey, perhaps? She walked slowly back to where the man she had come to visit waited. 'And what's all that about?' he wanted to know.

He was elderly and short and rather stout and her father's closest friend, and like him, was one of the Jurats of the island, perhaps the highest honour a citizen of Guernsey could aspire to. Victoria had known him all her life; when she had been a small girl and his wife had been alive, they had come frequently to her home, but now he was alone and although they saw him often, he seldom came to see them any more. Nevertheless, she knew that he was always delighted to see them. She looked at him with deep affection and said: 'Oh, nothing. Just that yacht, it seems such a daft sort of day to sail.'

'Well, as to that, it's a matter of who's sailing it, isn't it? It seemed to me that the boat was being handled by someone who knew what he was about. Do you know him?'

Victoria perched herself on the end of the wheelbarrow. 'No—yes, well, we met—just for a little while when I was out walking. I've no idea who he is.' She shrugged her shoulders and added falsely, 'And I don't really care.'

Mr Givaude, alias Uncle Gardener, lifted a face which bore strong traces of his Norman ancestors and stared at her rain-wet face. He didn't answer, only made a grunting sound and said: 'How about tea? It's early, but I've finished here. Come on up to the house.'

His home was tucked away to one side of the Prisoners' Walk, and although it was still early, as Mr Givaude had observed, his housekeeper was waiting for them, ready to take Victoria's wet anorak and then to bring in the tea-tray with the old silver teapot and the cherry cake she made so well. Victoria ate two generous slices while she told Uncle Gardener about hospital and how she hoped to get the ward within a year, and how beastly London was except when she went to the theatre or out to dinner, when it was the greatest possible fun.

'Want to live there for ever?' her companion asked.

'No,' she sounded positive about it.

'Then you'd better hurry up and find yourself a husband. After all, you're the eldest, you should have first pick.'

She grinned at him. 'And what chance do I have when the others are around?' she demanded. 'They're quite spectacular, you know. I only get noticed when I'm on my own.'

Her companion took a lump of sugar from the pot and scrunched it up.

'Bah,' he said roundly, 'fiddlesticks, I'll tell you something—I was out with your mother and father a little while ago and do you know what I heard someone say? They were talking about your sisters, and this person said: ''Maybe they do make the rest of the girls here look pretty dim, but wait until you've seen the eldest of 'em—and the best, a real smasher.'' What do you think of that?'

'Codswallop,' stated Victoria succinctly. 'It must have been someone who had never seen me—and anyway, Uncle Gardener, I don't care overmuch about being pretty.' She looked at him earnestly. 'I want to be liked—loved because I'm me, not just because I'm pretty.'

Mr Givaude nodded in agreement. 'Don't worry, Vicky,' he said, 'you will be.'

She went soon afterwards, mindful that she had to be home in good time, and with the promise that she would return to say goodbye before she went back to London. The rain had stopped and the clouds were parting reluctantly to allow a watery sunshine to filter through, probably it would be a fine day tomorrow. She walked quickly home, wondering what she should do with it— they could take the Mini if their mother didn't want it and go across the island to Rocquaine Bay; it was still early in the year, but on the western shores of the island it would be warm in the sheltered coves. She turned towards the town when she reached the end of the pier and instead of going along the Esplanade and up Havelet, turned off at the Town Church. At the corner, before she reached the shelter of the little town's main street she took a backward look at the sea. It was empty; her half-formed idea that the yacht with the brown sails might have turned and sailed back into harbour died almost before she became aware of it. All the same, that evening, sitting in the theatre waiting for the curtain to go up, she looked around her, just in case the stranger might be there too.

They went to Rocquaine Bay the next morning with Victoria driving. She wasn't a good driver, but she knew the island well, and most of the people on it; it wasn't like driving on the mainland where there was no one to give her a hand if she reversed down the wrong street or met a bus head-on. It was a grand morning with a wind which was going to strengthen later in the day and a pale sky from which a surprisingly warm sun shone. Victoria stopped the car when they reached Pleinmont Point and they all piled out and walked along the cliff path, past the radio station to the edge of the cliffs to get a view of the lighthouse. The keen air made them hungry and they were glad enough to stop at Portelet and have coffee and buns, arguing briskly among themselves as to whether it was worth leaving the car and walking back along the cliff path for a mile or so. They decided against it at last, although Victoria promised herself that when next she came on holiday she would walk from her home and swim in Venus's Pool and explore the Creux Mahie—a cave she hadn't visited for several years. Louise teased her gently about it.

'Honestly, Vicky,' she declared, 'there's heaps of other things to do. Who wants to poke round an old cave, and the water in the pool is cold until summer. When will you be home again?'

Victoria thought. 'Well, this is the last week of my holidays for this year—I start again in April. I think I'll try and get a week in May.'

'Don't forget we're all going to Scotland in September,' Amabel reminded her. 'That'll be two weeks. You're awfully lucky getting six weeks. Doctors aren't so lucky.'

There was a sympathetic murmur from her sisters;

Amabel and a newly qualified, overworked young doctor at the hospital had taken a fancy to each other. The affair was in its very early stages and the entire family were careful not to mention it unless Amabel brought the subject up.

'They do better as they get more senior,' said Victoria soothingly. 'And once they've got a practice...'

Amabel brightened and her sisters smiled at each other; they quarreled fiercely among themselves on occasion, but their affection for each other was just as fierce, and Amabel had the sweetest nature of them all.

'We'd better go,' suggested Victoria, and the other three rose at once because she was the eldest and although she couldn't match them in size she had always led them. It was when they were almost in St Peter Port again that Stephanie remembered that she had promised their mother to buy some fruit in the market, which naturally enough led Amabel to say that in that case she might as well pop into the arcade and see if they had got the belt she'd ordered.

'I'll come with you,' said Louise. She looked at Victoria, 'You don't mind, Vicky? We shall only be a minute or two.'

Victoria nodded and pulled into the side of the street, there wasn't much traffic about and even fewer pedestrians. She switched off the engine and said: 'Five minutes, and if you're not back you can jolly well walk home!'

She watched them cross the road and turn off in the direction of the arcades and the market. Even in slacks and sweaters and at a distance, they looked striking. When they were out of sight she stared idly around her. Across the street was the man who had been so much in her thoughts. His face was grave and unsmiling, which should have stopped her smiling at him but didn't.

He crossed the street slowly, almost as if he were reluctant to speak to her, but when he reached the car he said politely enough: 'Good morning. I hope you took no hurt from your wetting the other day?'

He still hadn't smiled and she found herself wishing that he would.

'No, thank you.' She felt curiously shy and was furious with herself for being so and presently when he didn't reply she added inanely: 'You're still here, then.'

The thick black brows were raised very slightly and he smiled suddenly and her heart lost its steady rhythm. She was still searching wildly for something interesting to talk about, something which would keep him there just a little longer, when someone whistled from across the street and he straightened up and looked over his shoulder and said: 'Ah, I see I'm wanted,' and added, 'Perhaps we shall meet again.'

His tone had been so formal that she thought it very unlikely; she watched him regain the opposite pavement and disappear, going up the hill, away from the sea-front, to join the little boy she had seen before, and this time the girl she had seen him with was there too. Victoria looked away. Oh, well, she thought, there must be a great many more men in the world like him, and knew it for cold comfort.

She didn't see him again for several days, not, in fact, until she was getting out of her father's car on the White Rock Pier, preparatory to boarding the boat back to Weymouth, on her way back to St Judd's. He was standing so close to the car that it was impossible to avoid him. She said: 'Oh, hullo,' and looked quickly away in case he should think that she might want to talk to him. Which she did very much indeed, but there was no fear of that, for by the time the rest of the Parsons family had got out of the car, he had disappeared, and for a little while at least she forgot about him while she said her goodbyes and went on board. It was the night boat, and although the boat was by no means full her father had insisted that she should have a cabin to herself. She felt grateful for this as she settled herself for a short night's sleep.

She would have breakfast on the train and get to London in time to go to dinner in the hospital if she wanted to. She hated going back; she always did, but she would be coming again in a couple of months. It was silly at her age to feel even faintly homesick. She switched her thoughts to St Judd's and kept them there despite an alarming tendency to allow the man she had met and would doubtless never meet again to creep into her head. Besides, she reminded herself firmly, he was married, and she was old-fashioned enough to believe that was sufficient reason to forget him. The highminded thought was tinged with sadness as she closed her eyes and went to sleep.

It was almost light when they docked at Weymouth. Victoria got into the waiting train and went along to breakfast and schooled her thoughts so well that by the time her taxi drew up outside the hospital, she had almost succeeded in forgetting him—but not quite.

CHAPTER TWO

THE brisk, instant routine of St Judd's was something Victoria almost welcomed, so that she could tell herself as frequently as possible that it was her life, the one she had chosen even though her parents had wanted her to stay at home, busying herself with voluntary work of some sort; indulging her talent for sketching while she waited for, and in due course married, some suitable man. She alone of their four daughters had rebelled against this pleasant tameness even while she suffered acute homesickness each time she returned to work. That she was more fortunate than many of her friends in hospital she freely admitted, for she didn't need to depend upon her salary; her father was generous so that she could make the long journey to Guernsey whenever she could manage her holiday. All the same she prized her independence, although she knew in her heart that while nursing satisfied her need to do something with her life, she would leave it at a moment's notice if she met a man she could love.

She went on duty the morning after her return, to find a ward whose inmates had changed very little during her week's absence. Sister Crow welcomed her back with the mixture of fussy grumbling and gossip to which Victoria had become accustomed. The staff nurse who had replaced Victoria had been most unsatisfactory—she had overslept; she had insisted on having a free evening on the very day Sister Crow hadn't wanted her to; she was, said Sister Crow crossly, far too modern.

Victoria, pouring out their morning coffee in Sister's

office, said gently: 'Staff Nurse Morgan's sweet with the patients, Sister, and so kind.'

Sister Crow bridled. 'That's as may be, Staff Nurse Parsons, but I for one am unable to understand the half of what she says—she is not good Ward Sister material.'

Victoria suppressed a strong desire to observe that perhaps Morgan didn't want to be a Ward Sister anyway; she was pretty and gay, and Victoria happened to know that her life was both full and lively, which probably accounted for her kindness and understanding of the patients under her care. But to say that to the Old Crow was merely to annoy her further and would do no one any good at all. She contented herself by saying:

'The patients liked her, Sister.'

Sister Crow stirred her coffee and remarked snappishly: 'They like you too, Staff Nurse, and you are a far better nurse. Much as I regret retiring from this ward I am at least satisfied that you, if given the opportunity, will carry on in a way worthy of the training I have given you.'

To which highminded speech Victoria could think of nothing to say, although the thought, completely unbidden, that perhaps she didn't want to be a Ward Sister after all did cross her mind, to be rejected as there was a knock on the door and Johnny Dawes, the medical houseman, came in followed by a tallish young man, good-looking and fair.

Johnny said politely: 'Good morning, Sister Crow, here's Doctor Blake, you met yesterday, didn't you?' He looked at Victoria. 'But I don't think that Staff and he have met yet?' He had half turned his back on the Old Crow as he spoke and gave Victoria a wink, for when that lady wasn't about he was apt to treat her staff nurse like one of his sisters—an attitude which Victoria found quite natural, but now, as Sister Crow was present, she replied formally: 'Good morning, Doctor Dawes. No, we haven't met.'

'The new RMO,' said Johnny, 'Doctor Jeremy Blake—Staff Nurse Parsons.'

She offered a hand and said, How do you do? and gave the new member of the staff a frank, friendly look. He seemed at first glance rather nice and very good-looking, although his mouth was a little too full for her taste and his eyes too pale a blue. Probably, she thought good-humouredly, he was weighing her up too and finding her not quite to his taste either. She got up and fetched two more cups; Sister Crow poured coffee and settled down to a ten-minute lecture on how to run a ward and, what was more important, how the members of the medical staff should behave on it. Victoria and Johnny had heard it all a great many times before, but Doctor Blake hadn't; he listened with polite attention and drank his coffee and when she paused for breath, suggested that a ward round might be a good idea. He looked at Victoria as he spoke and added: 'If you're busy, Sister, I'm sure Staff Nurse...'

'Staff Nurse has a great deal to do,' interrupted Sister Crow. 'I shall go with you myself, and you,' she finished, addressing Johnny, 'may come with me.'

That left Victoria to collect the coffee cups on to the tray, ready for Dora the ward maid, and then go along to the treatment room to make sure that the various injections had been drawn up correctly and then supervise their giving, before disappearing into the linen cupboard to check the clean linen, a task she loathed and considered a fearful waste of time. She preferred to be with the patients, but Sister Crow considered that the ward staff nurse should do all the duller administrative jobs. 'And that's something I'll change,' Victoria promised herself crossly as she counted sheets. But some of the crossness, although she wouldn't admit it, was disappointment at not doing a round with the new doctor, even though, upon reflection, she wasn't quite sure if she was going to like him.

She had a split duty that afternoon because the Old Crow wanted an evening. She hated splits; there was no time to do more than rush out for any necessary shopping, or if the weather was bad, sit for an hour or so in the sitting room, reading or writing letters. Splits weren't actually allowed, but they were sometimes inevitable and she seemed to collect more than her fair share—another thing she would put right when she had a ward of her own. She sat in front of the electric fire, writing home; she told them all about the new doctor, and all the while she was writing another image, quite a different one from that of Doctor Blake, kept dancing before her eyes. It was a relief when two of her friends came to join her, full of questions as to what she thought of the new RMO and what she had done on her holiday, a topic which naturally enough led to the more interesting one of clothes. They were all deep in this vital conversation when Victoria looked at her watch and exclaimed:

'Lord, look at the time—I'm on in half an hour! Come up to my room and I'll make some tea—I brought a cake back with me.'

The three of them repaired up the bare, clean staircase to the floor above where her room was, and being healthy and young and perpetually hungry, they demolished the cake between them.

Doctor Blake came again that evening as Victoria was sitting in the office writing up the Kardex. She looked up with faint surprise and some impatience as he came in, because she had got a little behind with her work and she wouldn't be ready for the night staff unless she kept at it. He must have seen the look, though, for he said reassuringly:

'Don't stop, I only came to read up some notes—it's the ward round tomorrow, isn't it, and I want to be quite sure of things.'

Victoria made a small sympathetic sound. 'Of course—behind you on the shelf, they're in alphabetical order,' and bent her bright head over her writing. She had turned over perhaps three cards when she became aware that he was staring at her. She finished writing 'Paracetamol' because it was a word she had to concentrate upon to get the spelling right and looked up.

'What's the matter?' she asked, 'Do you want something, or is my cap crooked?'

He smiled, his eyes like colourless glass. 'I can't help staring,' he said, 'you're so utterly lovely.'

She had been called lovely before by various young men; usually she accepted the compliment gracefully and without conceit, for it would have been foolish to pretend she wasn't pretty when she so obviously was. She had learnt at an early age to take her good looks as a matter of course—nice to have, but not vital to her happiness. But now for some reason she felt embarrassed and annoyed as well. He was almost a stranger and she hadn't liked the way he had said it; as though he had expected her to be pleased and flattered at his admiration. She said with a composure which quite hid her distaste:

'Thank you. Perhaps you would like to take the notes away with you? I have quite a lot of work to do still, and I daresay you have too.'

The annoyance on his face was so fleeting that she wasn't sure if she had imagined it. It was replaced at once by a smile. 'I've annoyed you, I'm sorry.' He got up and put the notes away. 'I'll come back later if I may.' His smile became apologetic. 'Don't hold it against me, will you?'

Victoria smiled too. Perhaps she had been too hasty in her judgement of him. 'No, of course not. Goodnight.'

Sir Keith Plummer's bi-weekly ward rounds were always a sore trial to Victoria, and she knew, the moment she set foot on the ward the next morning, that that day's was to prove no exception to the rule. Not only had one of the diabetics thrown away a valuable specimen and been unable to produce another in the short time left to him before the great man appeared, but Mr Bates, that most docile of patients, had decided to feel sick, so that instead of lying neatly in his bed he was sitting up apprehensively over a basin, and to add to all these trials two sets of notes had disappeared into thin air. Victoria had sent two of the nurses to look for them and dared them to return without these vital papers. 'Try Physio,' she whispered urgently so that Sister Crow shouldn't hear, 'and OPD; the Appointments Office, X-ray, anywhere—and for mercy's sake, be quick!'

They sidled in, a few yards ahead of Sir Keith and his retinue, and behind Sister Crow's back, shook their heads and rolled their eyes heavenwards, then melted away into the sluice as the ward doors opened and Sir Keith walked in. Victoria, from her station by bed number one, watched a routine which she knew by heart. Sir Keith stopped short just inside the doors and Sister Crow, who had been lurking in wait for him, advanced to his side so that they could exchange civil greetings before forming the procession which would presently wend its way up one side of the ward and down the other. It was a pity, thought Victoria, that the Old Crow had been trained so long ago that she regarded all consultants as gods and had made no move to change her views and treat them like anyone else. Victoria watched her standing with her head reverently bowed, listening to Sir Keith's pleasant voice rambling on, but the head came up with a jerk as the wretched student nurse Black, whose shoes squeaked, came out of the sluice, to retreat immediately under Sister Crow's threatening gaze. The same gaze hovered over Mr Payne, who had bronchitis, and Mr Church, who had asthma, daring either of them to allow a cough to disturb the utter quiet of the ward, and both gentlemen, anxious to please, lay rigid, their slowly empurpling faces bearing testimony to this fact. When at last human nature could stand no more, they coughed in such good earnest that Victoria was forced to leave her position with the exalted group around the consultant and fly to their aid. She had only just succeeded in quieting them both when there was a fresh disturbance, this time at the ward doors, and obedient to the indignant jerk of Sister Crow's head, Victoria sped silently down the ward. Some poor soul who had mistaken the visiting hours, she supposed, and saw at once how wrong she was. He looked different, of course, for he had exchanged his guernsey for a suit of clerical grey; her eyes took in its well-cut elegance and the exquisiteness of his tie as he advanced, with no sign of unease, to meet her.

She would have liked to have said hullo, but bearing in mind the Old Crow's dislike of any sound at all during the round she merely raised a cautionary finger to her lips and then pointed to the doors—a gesture to which he appeared to take exception, for he said without any effort at all to lower his voice: 'My dear girl, don't you try and send me away. I've had the devil's own job getting here in the first place.'

Victoria just stopped herself from wringing her hands. 'It's the round,' she hissed. 'Please wait outside, there's a chair on the landing.'

'Do I look as though I need to sit down?' he enquired with interest.

She conquered a strong desire to giggle, shook her head and said coldly: 'I must ask you to wait.'

He beamed at her. 'But I will, dear girl, I'll wait as long as you like.' He went on; 'You know, I liked you better with your hair down your back, even if you did look a bit of a fright.' She was still struggling to think of a dignified but quelling reply to this piece of impertinence when Sir Keith's voice, smooth and resonant, floated down the ward.

'There you are, dear fellow. Come and join us—I was beginning to think that you had found it impossible to come after all.'

He bent to say something to Sister Crow and the 'dear fellow', with a friendly pat on Victoria's outraged shoulder, advanced to the group of people by number six bed, and she, because it was expected of her, followed him, to take up her position just behind Sister, so that when that lady wanted notes or a tape measure or a tendon hammer to hand to Sir Keith, Victoria was there to supply them. Sir Keith put out a hand and said: 'Alexander, this is delightful, it seems a long time—Sister Crow, let me introduce Doctor van Schuylen, on a visit to this country. He's by way of being a specialist in chests.' He looked round the circle of faces. 'My RMO,' he went on, 'Doctor Blake, and my houseman, Doctor Dawes.' His gaze passed over the physiotherapist, his secretary and Victoria and rested on his patient, the hapless Mr Bates, his basin removed pro tem and looking very uneasy without it.

Victoria, handing X-rays, Path Lab forms and a pin to tickle the soles of Mr Bates' feet to see if he reacted in the proper manner, kept a wary eye on him; Sir Keith had most luckily finished with him and was about to move on to the next bed when Mr Bates went a little paler than he already was, so that she dropped her burden of forms and notes and made a beeline for the basin, but Doctor van Schuylen was ahead of her; he had it nicely in position under Mr Bates' pallid chin even as she reached him; he did it with a calm and matter-of-fact air which took no account of Sister Crow's horrified indrawn breath, waiting impassively until Nurse Black squeaked out of the sluice and took over, and only then did he relinquish the basin, giving that damsel—a small, plain girl known inevitably among her colleagues as Beauty—a smile of such charm that she smiled widely back at him.

He rejoined Sir Keith without a word, to be drawn instantly into a discussion on bronchiectiasis. Victoria listened to his deep, quiet voice, comparing it with Doctor Blake's. That gentleman, intent no doubt on impressing his chief, was holding forth at some length, addressing most of his observations to the Dutchman, in a manner which Victoria considered unnecessarily patronising, although their recipient apparently did not, for he lolled against the end of the bed with his hands in his pockets and his eyes fixed steadfastly upon Doctor Blake's face. It was only when that gentleman paused for breath that Sir Keith declared in a dry, gentle voice:

'My dear Blake, all that you have said is most admirable, but I must point out to you that you are taking coals to Newcastle, for our good friend here happens to be the author of the various papers you have been quoting at him.'

Victoria was forced to admire the way Doctor Blake bottled up his rage; he even managed a laughing apology to Doctor van Schuylen, his pale eyes colourless with a dislike he almost, but not quite concealed. She shivered

a little. He would be a bad enemy, she decided, studying
his good looks, and then transferred her gaze to Doctor
van Schuylen, still lolling, with a lazy, good-natured
smile upon his face, just as though he was taking the
other man's apologies at face value. Surely he could
see…? He turned to look at her and she realised that he
certainly had seen; his eyes, in such a placid face, were
very alert. She was so relieved that she smiled warmly
at him and Sister Crow, catching her at it, gave an indignant snort and commanded: 'Staff Nurse, be good
enough to ask someone from the Path Lab to come here
at once.' She accompanied this command with a heavy
frown. In her opinion, nurses—even staff nurses—did
not smile at consultants, nor for that matter at any
strange doctor who happened to turn up, especially the
kind of smile Victoria had just given.

Victoria, aware of the Old Crow's wrath, murmured:
'Certainly, Sister,' and went off down the ward and out
of its door and into the office to telephone, something
she did with dispatch and her usual competence, using
only a small part of her brain to do so; the rest of it was
deeply occupied by speculation upon Doctor van Schuylen's sudden appearance, his probable departure and
whether there was any likelihood of seeing more of him.
She went back to the ward presently, the missing notes,
which she had quite forgotten and which she had prov-
identially discovered on Sister's desk, under one arm.
She added them tidily to their fellows and took up her
station once more just behind Sister Crow without looking once at Doctor van Schuylen.

In fact, she studiously avoided his eye for the entire
round—a fairly easy matter as it turned out, for Sister
Crow saw to it that she was kept busy, and when the
slow procession had at last wound its way out of the
ward doors, Victoria, having made very certain that Dora

had the right number of cups on the tray, was instructed to go back into the ward and make sure that the patients' beds were tidied once more.

'But have your coffee first, Staff Nurse,' the Old Crow invited, and looked at the clock as she spoke so that Victoria would know that she had observed the time and would expect her back in ten minutes exactly.

Victoria, once in the main corridor, flew down it at a good speed; she seldom went to coffee break, for it was usual for the staff nurses to have coffee with Sisters on the ward, but on round days Sister Crow didn't want her, and anyway, Victoria admitted fairly, the office didn't accommodate more than four people in comfort and the Old Crow disliked people sitting on the floor or perching on the sides of her desk. The dining room was only half full, but there were several of her friends gathered round a table in a corner. She joined them with an eye on the clock as she did so. 'Ten minutes,' she exclaimed breathlessly, 'Sister Crow made a note of it as I left.'

Kitty Blane from Women's Medical groaned in sympathy. 'I don't know how you stand her!' She filled a mug and pushed it across the table to Victoria. 'How did the round go? What do you think of our Jeremy?'

Victoria blew on her coffee to cool it. 'He's all right, I suppose.' She sounded doubtful. 'I don't know anything about him yet. He's good-looking...'

'Talking of good looks, did you get a sight of a tall dark and handsome stranger up your way? He came sauntering into ours about an hour ago and when I asked him what he wanted he said he was looking for Sir Keith Plummer, and when I told him where he was, he said: "Oh, yes—is that where the staff nurse has long bronze hair?" Someone you know, Vicky?'

'Well, not really,' said Victoria calmly, covering sudden feelings which weren't calm at all. 'Perhaps he mistook me for someone else.' Even while she spoke she wondered how he had found out that she worked on Men's Medical or if it had been coincidence. The latter, she decided, for was he not almost for certain a married man and had he at any time shown interest in her? Not to speak of. She grinned ruefully and Bunny Coles from Cas. asked:

'Fed up, Vicky? I'm not surprised with the Old Crow always fussing around. When are you off?'

'Five.' Victoria put down her mug. 'I must fly, you know what she is—all the beds to be tidy by the time she comes out of the office.' She made a face. 'So long, girls.'

There was no sign of anyone as she went back along the corridor and past Sister's office, although there was a murmur of voices and a sudden burst of laughter. Sir Keith must have made a joke, for that was the only time Sister Crow laughed about anything. Victoria went into the ward, sent all but one nurse to their coffee and started to straighten the beds and to get out of bed all those patients who had been kept in them for the round. She had reached Mr Bates and had sent Nurse Black to fetch a cool drink for the still queasy old man when the ward door was swung open with a good deal of vigour and a firm footfall trod towards her. She knew who it was, of course, and turned to face him as he fetched up within a few inches of her. He said without preamble: 'You're off at five. I'll be outside at five-thirty—no, five-forty-five, you'll want to do that hair of yours. I should like to take you out.'

She stared at him speechlessly, delight and doubt warring with each other in her lovely face, and before she could reply Mr Bates answered for her in his dry old voice.

'That's right, you go, Staff. Have a bit of fun, yer must feel like it after the whole day here with the likes of us.'

'No,' said Victoria with a firmness denied by her eyes, 'thank you.'

'Why not?'

She glanced at Mr Bates, who said at once, 'Cor, luv a duck, Staff, I'm stone deaf—can't 'ear a word.'

She smiled at him. He'd been in number six bed for so long and he was really an old dear; all the same, she half turned away from him to say in a low voice: 'You see, I don't go out—with m-married men.'

'Very laudable,' commented Doctor van Schuylen approvingly. 'Shall we make it five-thirty and never mind the hair?'

She raised enormous tawny eyes fringed with curling dark lashes and met his blue ones. There was a glint in them which made her blink and falter. 'You are married?'

'No,' he answered coolly, 'not yet.' He said nothing further, only looked amused, and it was so obvious that he was awaiting an explanation that she began to explain. 'Oh—well, you see you were dining with someone and she had a wedding ring, and the next day you had a little boy with you, and then I saw you with them...'

It was impossible to know what he was thinking, for his voice was as bland as his face and his eyes were almost covered by suddenly drooping lids.

'Ah, yes—of course. A natural mistake, but a mistake. Shall we say half past five?'

The ward door was pushed open and allowed to close with a minimum of noise—Sister Crow. Victoria's eyes met the Dutchman's and Mr Bates said happily: 'I ain't 'eard a word, but 'ave a nice evening of it, the two of yer.'

'Half past five,' breathed Victoria, and began on Mr Bates all over again while she listened to the doctor, skilfully and with great charm, draw a variety of red herrings across the Old Crow's path so that by the time she eventually reached Victoria she had quite forgotten why she had come into the ward.

Sister Crow had wanted an afternoon; Victoria, working through seemingly endless hours, prayed that she would come on duty as punctually as she usually did. She had been foolish, she decided as she prepared the medicine trolley for Sister's use later on, to say half past five, for she would almost certainly be late, and supposing he didn't wait? Supposing he were impatient? She contradicted herself; he wasn't an impatient man, of that she was quite certain, although for the life of her she couldn't guess how she knew that. She smiled with relief at the thought and Major Cooper, whom she was hauling back into bed after his afternoon exercises, stared at her.

'What the devil have you got to smile about?' he demanded irascibly. He was an ill-tempered old gentleman; that anybody would be otherwise was something he would not condone. Victoria had no intention of telling him, so instead she asked: 'What do you think of the Government's intention...'

It was a safe and sure red herring; he seized upon it and grumbled happily while she worked him out of his dressing gown and pulled on the woolly bedsocks he insisted upon wearing, and since she had heard it all before, it left her free to devote the greater part of her mind to the important question of what to wear that evening.

It was twenty minutes to six as she crossed the hospital entrance hall. The Old Crow had been punctual, but she had been chatty too, and it was all of a quarter past five by the time Victoria had got away. It was impossible to go to tea, and dinner, if that was the meal she hoped the doctor was inviting her to, was several hours off. She drank a glass of water from her toothmug and started tearing off her clothes. Luckily the bathrooms were empty and very few of her friends were about, and those who tried to engage her in conversation were told 'No time', and swept on one side. She was kneeling before the mirror in her room, because there were no stools before the dressing tables in the Home, putting her hair up very carefully, when the staff nurse on Children's came in with a cup of tea. 'Leave it if you haven't time,' she advised, 'but I bet you didn't get any—who's the date?'

Victoria, her mouth pursed over hair-grips, made sounds indicative of not telling, but her friend disregarded them. 'We think it's the foreign doctor who went to Kitty's ward.'

Victoria, having disposed of the grips, swallowed half a cup of tea.

'Yes—well, we met while I was home—and don't,' she went on severely, 'start any ideas. He's only asked me out because he happened to meet me again—you know, being polite.'

She was wriggling into her dress—a very plain cinnamon-coloured wool—and her friend obligingly zipped her up the back before she spoke.

'Why should he have to be polite?' she asked forthrightly. 'I've never met a man yet who asked a girl out unless he wanted to.'

Victoria was head and shoulders inside the wardrobe and her voice was muffled. 'Maybe he wants someone to listen to him while he talks,' she suggested, and hoped not. She slid into the matching topcoat and dug her feet into brown patent shoes which had cost her a small fortune and flew to the door, snatching up her handbag as she went. 'See you,' she said briefly, and hurried down-stairs.

He was leaning against the little window behind which Smith, the head porter, sat, enjoying a chat, but when he saw her he came to meet her across the lino-leumed floor and without giving her a chance to say that she was sorry that she was late, swept her outside and across the forecourt to where a Mercedes-Benz 350SL coupé was standing. It had, Victoria's sharp eyes no-ticed, a Dutch number-plate.

'It is yours?' she wanted to know as he opened the door for her to get in.

'Yes.' He shut her in with an almost silent snap of the handle and went round to his own seat.

'You didn't have it in Guernsey.'

'No.' He was sitting beside her now. 'What a girl you are, always asking questions!'

'I never—' she began, and then remembered that she had asked him quite a lot and closed her pretty mouth firmly, thinking better of it.

'Have you had tea?' His voice was pleasantly friendly.

'No—that is, I had some in a mug while I was chang-ing.'

He nodded with the air of a man who was in the habit of drinking his own tea in such a manner. 'I've brought a picnic basket with me, I thought we might run a little way out of town and have tea in the car and then go on somewhere for dinner.' He glanced sideways at her and smiled. 'Unless there's something else you would rather do?'

There was nothing else that she would rather do; she said so.

'Good—let's go, then.'

It was the evening rush hour; she was relieved to find that not only did he drive very well indeed; he displayed none of the irritation or impatience she had come to expect from anyone negotiating London at such times; moreover he talked as he drove, an unhurried flow of smalltalk which put her at her ease. St Judd's was in the East End, or almost so. He had left that part of the city far behind and was across the river, travelling in a south-western direction when she remarked: 'You know London very well.'

'You sound surprised.' He didn't give her any reason, though, but went on: 'There's a quiet pub at Abinger, we'll go down through Leatherhead and turn off as soon as we can find a reasonably quiet spot for tea, and then go on to Abinger Hammer. I presume you don't have to be in at ten o'clock or whenever you have your curfew.'

Victoria chuckled. 'I'm exempt. Once we're trained we're allowed to stay out until a reasonable hour.'

He said 'Good' as he edged the car past a loaded van and then a string of slow-moving cars, and after a minute or two when it became apparent that he wasn't going to say anything else for the time being, Victoria ventured: 'Was it just...I mean, were you surprised to see me?'

'I'm surprised each time I set eyes on you—you're very lovely. You must get a little bored with being told that by all the men you meet.'

She remembered the last man to say that to her, Doctor Blake, and how she had hated it, yet now she was glowing with delight. She said with admirable calm: 'It's according to who says it, and if I were with my sisters no one would think of saying any such thing—they're beautiful.'

He glanced at her. 'Yes, they are.' He turned the car off into a side road whose signpost said Walton-on-the-Hill, but after half a mile he turned it again, this time into a mere lane, saying: 'Somewhere here, I should think, wouldn't you? I'm not quite sure where we are, but we can look at the map presently.'

It was quiet and the late afternoon had brought a wintry nip with it. The doctor stretched behind him and produced a tea basket from the back of the car. 'Do you want to stay in the car or shall we try outside?' he enquired.

'Outside,' said Victoria promptly. 'We can always get back in if it gets too cold, can't we?' She looked around her. 'Look, there's a little hollow there under the hedge, it shouldn't be too bad.' She looked up at him, laughing. 'It's fun, isn't it, having a picnic tea at half past six in a dropping temperature?'

He laughed too as he got out to open her door and help her out and picked up the basket. 'Yes,' he said slowly, 'but I fancy anything with you would be fun, Victoria.'

They had reached the little hollow and she stood looking down at her shoes, conscious of her quickened heartbeats. She said rather shyly:

'It was strange that we should meet again,' and looked at him startled when he gave a great rumble of laughter.

'No,' he said, still laughing, 'not strange at all. I had this meeting arranged with Sir Keith Plummer; I had seen you board the boat for Weymouth and I heard your mother telling you to be sure and have breakfast on the train. I gambled on it being the London train and I already knew that you were a nurse.'

'Oh? How?'

'My friends knew someone who knows your father. It was only a question of enquiring at the London hospitals.'

She gaped at him. 'You mean you didn't know I was at St Judd's? But you asked Kitty if there was a copper-headed nurse...'

He stared back at her, his eyes glinting with amusement. 'I had resigned myself to visiting each hospital in turn, but luck was on my side, wasn't it? You were in the very first one, and one, moreover, in which I have every right to be.' He spread a rug on the bank and put the basket beside it and observed placidly: 'You must be dying for your tea. Sit down and we'll have it now or we shan't have an appetite for dinner.'

Victoria sat down with the speechless obedience of a little girl while she sorted out the muddled thoughts surging around her head.

'Why did you do it?' she enquired at length.

He opened the hamper and took out the flask of tea and two cups as well as a variety of tidily wrapped sandwiches. He undid them, poured the tea, added milk and sugar, handed her a cup and proffered one of the packets, with the remark that the sandwiches were cucumber. She took one mechanically, feeling a little breathless and at a complete loss, an experience she had until then not had. She took a bite and drank some tea. 'I still don't see why...' she began.

'No? Never mind, let's enjoy ourselves and be glad that we have been fortunate enough to meet again. Tell me about your work.'

He sounded like a big brother or a kindly uncle; she tidied away her disturbing, exciting thoughts and told him while he plied her with delicate sandwiches and little cakes and tea, which even from a thermos tasted delicious. He didn't eat much himself, but Victoria hardly noticed that, for she was telling him all about the hospital and why she had trained as a nurse and how much she loved her home, but presently she came to a stop, peered at him through the gloom and asked: 'And you? What part of Holland do you come from, and are you going to be in England long?'

'The Hague. I have a practice there, though my home is just outside—in Wassenaar. My parents live in Leiden, my father is a doctor but more or less retired—he does consulting work and sits on various committees, and when I am away, as I am from time to time, he helps out with my practice. I have two brothers and two sisters, all younger than I, and all married.' He paused and she knew that he was smiling at her through the dusk. 'There, have I not answered all your questions before you could ask them?'

'No—well, that is, almost. Are you here to lecture or were you on holiday in Guernsey?'

'I'm here for a few days before I go up to Birmingham and Edinburgh and then back home. I was on holiday in Guernsey—I have friends there.'

Victoria started to re-pack the hamper. 'You must be very clever,' she began, 'to lecture, you know. Are you older than you look?'

She heard his rumble of laughter. 'That's a difficult question, for I have no idea how I look, have I?' He leaned over and fastened the tea basket and put out a hand to help her to her feet. 'I'm thirty-five, give or take a month or two—almost eleven years older than you.'

She stopped in her tracks. 'How did you know that?'

'Oh, a friend of a friend, you know.' His voice sounded casual as he opened the car door for her and then went to put the tea things in the boot. In the car beside her again he looked at his watch. 'I booked a table for eight o'clock—supposing we cut down behind Hindhead and circle back?'

'That would be nice, Doctor…'

'My name's Alexander,' he prompted her mildly. 'You may have noticed that I call you Victoria, for I find myself quite unable to address you as Miss Parsons. What are your sisters' names?'

Victoria told him; she told him how old they were too and what they did with their days and how clever Amabel was with her sketching and what a formidable couple Stephanie and Louise were on the tennis court. One thing led to another; by the time they arrived at the Abinger Hammer, she had told him a great deal without being aware of it; it was only afterwards she realised that he had told her only the barest facts about himself.

They had leisurely drinks in the bar of the peaceful old pub and dined off Chicken Savoyarde, followed by chocolate roulade washed down with white burgundy. They went back into the bar for their coffee, sitting at a little table in the now crowded room with so much to talk about that they hardly noticed the cheerful noise around them. It was only when the landlord called, 'Time, gentlemen, please,' that Victoria broke off in mid-sentence. 'It can't be as late as that already,' she exclaimed. 'We've never been here as long as that?'

Doctor van Schuylen laughed. 'Indeed we have. Are you in a hurry to get back?'

'No—' She paused. 'That is, I mustn't be too late because I'm on in the morning and I must make up a clean cap...'

He laughed again and she flashed at him: 'That sounds like a silly excuse, but it isn't.'

He stared at her across the table. The gleam in his eyes could have been amusement, she didn't know, but perhaps it wasn't after all, for he said gravely: 'I know it isn't, Victoria, I know you well enough for that.' He smiled gently at her and her heart rocked against her ribs.

'I shall take you straight back and you shall make up your cap and have your beauty sleep—not,' he added softly, 'that you need it.'

'Oh, I do,' she contradicted him, 'it's been quite a day on the ward.'

Just as though she hadn't spoken, he added: 'You're beautiful enough as it is.'

She got into the car wordlessly. That was the second time he had called her beautiful and she was astonished at the delight she felt—just as though he were the first man ever to have said so. She considered the idea for a moment; he was the first man—none of the other men counted any more.

She was rather quiet on the trip back because she had a good deal to think about, but he didn't seem to notice, rambling on in a placid fashion about topics which must have been of so little importance that she was unable to remember anything about them later, only the pleasant sound of his voice—a quiet, calm voice, and deep. She liked listening to it.

They arrived back at St Judd's just before midnight and although she hastened to say: 'Don't get out—I'm going through the hospital to the Home,' he ignored her and got out too and walked with her to the big front doors. When she thanked him for her evening he said:

'It was delightful—I shall remember it while I'm away.'

'Oh yes.' She felt bereft. 'Birmingham and Edinburgh.'

He nodded without speaking and after a moment she put out a hand.

'Well, goodbye, Alexander. I hope you have a good trip. I don't know Birmingham, but Edinburgh's beautiful and there's a lot to see.'

'You know it? So do I—I've an Edinburgh degree.'

He was still holding her hand and when she pulled on it gently he merely tightened his grip and said: 'I shan't have much time for sightseeing, I must get back to Holland as soon as possible.'

'Yes, of course.' She made her voice sound coolly friendly, for after all, what was theirs but a casual meeting? And this time he let her hand go. She said, maintaining the coolness with difficulty: 'Well, goodbye, and thank you again,' then whisked through the door and across the hall and out of sight of him.

If Victoria wanted to forget him, she had no chance; her friends, during the next few days, saw to that, for they wanted to know every detail of her evening with him and then fell to discussing him at length and often, and when Tilly had exclaimed: 'He turns me on,' Victoria had felt a pang in her chest which was almost physical and no amount of reasonable thinking could dispel him entirely from her thoughts. After the first day or so she managed to convince herself that he had gone for good. There must be girls enough for him to choose from if he wanted an evening out; probably he had forgotten her already—a sensible thought which did nothing to dispel a sense of loss which bewildered her. She worked a little harder in order to get rid of it and when Doctor Blake invited her to go to the cinema with him, she accepted, although she wasn't really keen on going.

Jeremy Blake had behaved well, rather to her surprise, for he struck her as being a young man conceited enough to expect a quick conquest of any girl he cast his eyes upon, but beyond an attempt to hold her hand in the cinema which she parried without difficulty, he did nothing to which she could take exception, and when she was bidding him goodnight at the door of the Nurses' Home with a rather brisk thank you, he had been equally casual. She had gone up to her room convinced that she had been mistaken about him after all—he was really not too bad and certainly not the wolf she had suspected.

His behaviour bore out her opinion during the subsequent days—he was friendly in a casual way both on the ward and when they met outside it, and when Ellen, the night staff nurse and one of Victoria's closest friends, remarked one morning after she had given the report that she didn't fancy him at all, Victoria had felt impelled to defend him.

'He's quite nice,' she remarked. 'I didn't think I was going to like him, but he's quiet and just friendly.'

Ellen sauntered towards the door. 'As long as he stays that way,' she said darkly.

It was two days later that he asked Victoria to go out with him again and she refused. Afterwards she didn't know why she had done so, for he had proved a pleasant enough companion when they had gone to the cinema. Perhaps it was because he had suggested that they should go to a little club he knew of in Chelsea and dance that she had refused so promptly. He had said nothing, only shrugged his shoulders and said carelessly: 'Another time, perhaps,' but his eyes had seemed paler than ever even though he was smiling.

She hardly thought about him during the day; they were busy and although he came on to the ward several times, the only speech they had was to do with the patients.

She met him on the way off duty that evening. Men's Medical was on the top floor, reached by a bleak corridor of the narrow, dreary type so beloved by mid-Victorian architects of hospitals. It ran through most of the wing and then turned at right angles to continue on its way to an equally bleak staircase. It was depressing, with margarine-coloured walls and mud-coloured linoleum, polished to within an inch of its life. Victoria was perhaps halfway down this miserable passage when Jeremy Blake appeared around the corner ahead of her. He was walking very fast and she supposed him to be on his way to the ward, but when he drew level with her he stopped suddenly and caught her round the waist.

'And what do you think you're doing?' she demanded in a voice chilled with angry surprise.

'Oh, come off it, Vicky, you don't have to play the little lady with me.'

He laughed at her and for answer she attempted to remove his hands, but he only went on laughing and pulled her closer. 'We could have fun together.'

'I can think of nothing less likely,' she retorted indignantly. His face was only inches from hers and although he smiled his eyes glittered and his mouth looked mean. 'Let go!' she ordered him furiously. 'I don't want to go out with you, I said so and I meant it, and I certainly wouldn't want to go out with you again or have anything more to do with you!'

She lifted a capable hand, doubled into a fist, and pummelled his chest.

'Playing hard to get?' he wanted to know. 'Shall I tell you something, girlie? I always get a bird if I want her, and here's something on account.'

His face was very close. Victoria lifted a foot, neatly shod in its hospital regulation lace-up, and kicked his shin, and he loosened his hold. In a flash she was away, making for the bend in the passage. Once round it the stairs would be in sight and there might be someone about...

He caught up with her a couple of feet from the corner and clamped his hand on to her shoulders and forced her to a halt, turning her around to face him, but not without difficulty because she was a strong girl, then putting a hand under her chin to force her face up to his. 'You spitfire,' his voice was soft and unpleasant, 'now you've fooled about enough!'

She couldn't move her head, his hand was too strong. 'I'll scream!' She spoke with spirit and stopped at his smile.

'And a lot of good that will do you—you see, I shall say that I found you hysterical on my way to the ward, and you won't stand a chance, my dear. I've done it before and it always works...' He broke off, his smile frozen.

'Er—so sorry to interrupt,' said Doctor van Schuylen gently from somewhere behind her left ear, 'but I think you've got it wrong, my dear fellow.'

Victoria felt his hand, gentle and strong, on her waist and the next moment she had been whisked to one side, allowing the doctor just enough room to knock Doctor Blake down, having done which he dusted his hands off carefully, turned his back on the prostrate form and said with an air of calm, 'Hullo'. The smile he gave her was so kind that she would have liked to have burst into tears, but before she could do so he went on: 'I wondered if we might go out to dinner—somewhere gay where we can dance.' He was walking her round the corner and down the stairs as he spoke, and at the bottom Victoria stopped and put out a hand to touch his well-tailored sleeve almost timidly.

'I must explain,' she began, but was stopped by his quiet voice.

'Not a word, Victoria, or I might be tempted to go back and knock the fellow down again.'

She was very sure he meant it. 'Are you angry? He'll be all right, won't he?'

She felt it was a foolish question, but he stopped then, right outside Women's Surgical where one of the Office Sisters was taking the report from Sister Kennedy. He said simply: 'Yes, I'm angry, but don't worry, I have an excellent control over my temper and he's not much hurt, I believe.' He smiled at her and she found herself smiling back. 'I'll be very quick,' she assured him. 'What time will you come for me?'

He looked at his watch. 'Seven sharp—I must go back to the hotel and put on a black tie.' He took her hand and held it for a moment in his and didn't let it go when the Office Sister walked towards them. She wished them a civil good evening, looking at them with purposeful vagueness which Victoria found rather touching. She liked Office Sister, who was a widow with grown-up children, so that she treated the nurses rather in the same manner as she would have used towards her own children, and was loved for it.

When she had gone, Alexander gave her back her hand. 'I'll come with you as far as the Home,' he stated calmly. 'Do you mind where we go this evening?'

Victoria shook her head. She would have been quite happy sitting in a Wimpy Bar with him for the whole evening. At the Home door she tried to thank him again and he said: 'No, Victoria, there's no need to say any more—I'm only sorry I wasn't there a few minutes sooner.'

She had her hand on the door handle. 'I kicked him on the shin,' she observed with belated satisfaction.

She was looking at him as she spoke and he smiled: 'That's my girl!'

Victoria went on staring at him. That was exactly what she was and she had only just discovered it. His girl— for ever and ever and nothing could change that. She had often wondered what it would feel like to fall in love—really in love—and now she had, suddenly. It left her bewildered and uncertain and wildly happy. She gave him a dazzling smile, repeated 'Seven o'clock', and went through the door.

CHAPTER THREE

VICTORIA wasted ten minutes just sitting on the edge of her bed. For part of that time she didn't even think, only allowed her head to fill with delightful fairy stories with happy endings, but these gradually faded before common sense. That she was in love with Doctor van Schuylen she didn't dispute, but whether he felt the same about her was another matter. She was a pretty girl, but there were other girls just as pretty—moreover, he had two countries to choose from—there might be someone in Holland. And although he had come to her aid just at the right moment that evening, he would probably have done just the same for the Old Crow. She was momentarily diverted by the picture of Sister Crow repulsing Jeremy Blake, then felt mean, because the poor Old Crow must have been rather pretty when she was young—and then allowed her thoughts to return to her own problems. She would find out during the course of the evening if he was staying in London—she did a little arithmetic on her fingers; he had been gone for six days, surely time enough to go to Edinburgh as well as Birmingham, but perhaps he was on his way to Holland. It was a depressing thought, but there was nothing much she could do about it. She went to run a bath, dismissed her gloomy speculations and allowed herself to dwell on the coming delights of the evening.

She wore the prettiest dress she had—peacock blue silk with a wide skirt and great leg o' mutton sleeves gathered into long narrow cuffs fastened with pearl buttons; its small bodice had little pearl buttons marching down its front too, and its scooped-out neckline was exactly right for the pearl necklace her parents had given her for her twenty-first birthday. Victoria fastened it with care, got into her slippers, caught up her velvet evening cape and handbag and hurried downstairs. It was exactly seven o'clock. She slowed down in the hall. Perhaps she shouldn't have been quite so punctual, it made her look so eager, and now she felt shy as well. She put a hand up to her hair to make sure it was securely pinned and went to the door. Alexander was waiting there and she was glad of the dim light in the hall because the sight of him, elegant and very much at ease in a dinner jacket, made her feel almost giddy.

He helped her into the car and got in beside her. 'I'm glad you're on time,' his voice was casually friendly. 'I thought it would be nice to go through the parks—there won't be much traffic about.'

'Yes,' she was annoyingly breathless, 'that would be pleasant.' She watched the large hands on the wheel as he started the car. 'When did you get back?' she asked, 'and was it successful?'

'This afternoon about half past four, and yes, I believe it was tolerably successful—a pooling of ideas, you understand—it's amazing what we can learn from each other.'

They were travelling slowly through the muddled East End traffic and when he pulled up to allow a transport wagon to come out of a side street she said: 'Alexander, I went out with Jeremy Blake last week—to the cinema.' Even as she said it, it sounded silly in her ears. Why should she tell him she had been out with Jeremy? After all, she was free to go out with whom she pleased.

She caught his quick smile. 'I went out too—with one of the secretaries, a nice girl.'

'Was she pretty?'

He inched the car forward. 'I don't remember,' he spoke quietly and she knew that he meant it. 'I was lonely; I wanted to telephone you, write to you, even get into the car and come back and see you.'

She glowed. 'Oh, I was lonely too, that's why I went out with Jeremy. I thought it might pass the time.'

His voice was gentle. 'Why are you telling me this, Victoria?'

She had no idea, she was appalled when she thought about it; being in love with him had gone to her head and she was behaving like an idiot. She said in a stiff little voice: 'It—it just came into my head. It's a change from talking about the weather, isn't it?' And heard his chuckle even though he most annoyingly didn't answer her.

They didn't speak again until he turned the car into Hyde Park, to draw up presently and switch off the engine. He turned to look at her then and she saw the approval in his eyes and the admiration. 'Delightful,' he told her in his pleasant voice, 'and you smell like a flower garden.'

Victoria smiled a little; she had felt wildly extravagant in Guernsey buying such a large bottle of Roger et Gallet's Jeu d'Eau, and wished now that she had bought an even larger size. She wondered with pleasurable excitement what he was going to say next and was keenly disappointed when he asked: 'You don't mind if I smoke?'

'Please do,' she achieved the two words with a commendable sweetness and watched him go about the business of filling and lighting his pipe which he did with deliberation. It was only when he had got it going to his satisfaction that he spoke again.

'I've been looking forward to this,' he remarked, an observation which Victoria found difficult to answer although she longed to tell him that she had been longing to see him too. She was startled when he asked: 'Have you?'

She opened her little brocade bag and closed it again before she said carefully: 'Well, I couldn't look forward to something I didn't know was going to happen, could I?'

He gave her a long look. 'You knew that I should come back.'

She opened her bag again, looked at its contents and closed it. 'Yes, I think I did.'

'You know you did.'

How persistent the man was! 'All right, I knew,' she reiterated, quite put out. Her fingers were on the bag again when his hand came down to cover hers. His voice was gentle. 'Don't be scared, dear girl.'

Victoria looked at him then, her eyes wide. 'Scared? I've never been scared of anyone yet, least of all you.'

'I'm glad, although that isn't quite what I meant.' He smiled, a wholly friendly smile, and took his hand away. 'How's the ward?' he asked, and she switched back to the safe gossip of her daily life almost thankfully, then listened while he told her about his trip to Birmingham.

It was almost dark when he knocked out his pipe and said: 'How about our meal? I've booked a table for eight o'clock.' He started the car and she sat quietly beside him, thinking how like him it was not to mention anything about the unfortunate episode in the corridor. Briefly she wondered if Jeremy Blake was hurt and then forgot all about him, for they had stopped outside the Ritz Hotel and Alexander was helping her out and saying easily: 'We can have a drink first, if you'd care to.'

She had never been to the Ritz before. She agreed to meet him in the bar and went away to repair the ravages of sitting in the car for a half hour or so. She re-did her

face a little, inspected her person, tidied her hair and
concluded, rightly, that the dress suited her and that her
appearance was as immaculate as it was possible to be.
She swept into the bar presently and was rewarded by
the discreet stares of several gentlemen of whom she was
only vaguely aware, because Alexander was coming to
meet her.

They drank Pernod and talked about their childhood
and Alexander, for the first time, told her a little about
himself, she was so engrossed that it seemed an annoy-
ing interruption when the waiter came to tell that their
table was ready. They had eaten their hors d'oeuvres
when they decided to dance. Victoria, who danced very
well, discovered that Alexander danced well too; as the
evening wore on, what with the wine she had drunk with
the sole which followed the hors d'oeuvres, and the fillet
steak which came after that and the delightful surround-
ings, the band and above all, Alexander's company, Victoria was very happy indeed. It was while they were
dancing towards the end of the evening that he told her
that he was going away the following day, and the happiness was swallowed by an aching lump in her throat
which rendered her speechless. After a few moments she
achieved: 'Oh, are you?' It was rather muffled because
she had spoken into his shirt front—presently she would
be able to look at him and smile, but not yet.

'To Edinburgh,' he continued. 'I shall be gone for a
week. I shall be staying the night in London on my way
back to Holland. Could you get a week's holiday?'

Victoria looked at him then. 'A week's holiday,' she
repeated, bemused.

'Yes—I'm coming back to England in two weeks'
time—I have to go home for a week first. I thought we
might go over to Guernsey—your people will be there?'

She managed to say 'Yes', and added doubtfully: 'I

don't think I can get a week—it's a bit soon, but I shall be due a weekend...'

'Splendid.' He looked his usual calm and placid self; his voice was placid too, but there was a gleam in his eyes which completely melted the lump; she smiled widely and he said rather quickly: 'And now supposing we finish our dinner?'

They ate Pesche Ripiene—peaches stuffed with macaroons and almonds and candied orange peel, soaked in wine and baked and as a last delight, treated to a touch of Cointreau. Victoria hadn't eaten it before; it seemed exactly right for her happy mood. She gobbled it up daintily and said: 'Do let's dance again,' and when they were on the floor, 'Where will you stay?'

It seemed he knew what she was talking about. 'With my friends—you saw me with them, but I shall come for you each day as early as you can manage to get up. You'll do that?'

She nodded.

'And go to bed late?'

She nodded again and felt his hold on her tighten, although when he spoke his voice was mild. 'Let's go back to our table and get the dates fixed, shall we? And then I am going to take you back to the Home.'

The church clock close to St Judd's struck once as Alexander brought the Mercedes to a quiet halt. Victoria said: 'Don't get out, there's no need,' but might just as well have held her tongue. They walked together through the empty entrance hall, saying goodnight to the porter peering at them from his little window, and continued their way through the various corridors which would lead them to the quadrangle. It was quiet as they walked, so that the distant feet of hurrying nurses and the coughs and night noises from the wards seemed unnaturally loud. At the door they paused while the doctor threw it open on to the chilly spring night. The hospital loomed on three sides of them. The noises which had seemed loud before seemed even louder, coming from all around them, and on the top floor, where the theatre was, there were brightly lighted windows and they could hear the hiss of steam and the clatter of bowls. Victoria, snug in her own happy little world, spared a thought for whoever was on duty there as well as for the patient. Anxious to prolong the moment, she murmured: 'They're busy. When do you leave for Scotland?' and was taken aback by his answer. 'As soon as I've changed my clothes.'

'You mean now—right away?'

He smiled down at her. 'Why not? I have to be in Edinburgh by two o'clock. If I start within the next hour or so that will give me time to go to my hotel and have a meal.'

'But you should have gone earlier—you'll have no sleep. It's hundreds of miles. Why didn't you tell me?'

She was stopped by his quiet: 'Don't fuss, dear girl. What is a night's sleep or a few hundred miles? I'll be back in a week.'

'Yes. Thank you for a lovely evening, Alexander.' Her voice sounded stiff in her own ears, and she wondered how it sounded to him, but for the life of her she couldn't think of anything else to say, but it didn't seem to matter, for he caught her close and kissed her on her mouth.

'Our lovely evening,' he corrected her, and pushed her gently through the doorway where he stood watching her until she reached the Home on the other side of the quadrangle. She turned and waved before she went inside and he lifted a hand in salute.

The week seemed a year, although she was unendingly busy. There had been a mini 'flu epidemic; easy enough to weather if one was young and healthy but hard on the older ones. The ward filled fast with elderly gentlemen who protested their fitness between bouts of coughing. Victoria, sprinting up and down the ward with her syringes of antibiotics and the inhalations Sir Keith believed in, had little time to pine, let alone think, for the incoming patients brought their germs with them so that some of the patients who had been in the ward for some time became infected too. Just the same, she managed to find time to ask Sister if she could have her long weekend, much to that lady's annoyance.

'You've only just come back,' protested the Old Crow. 'You modern girls, you're all so restless, flitting from here to there...'

'I'm only going home for three days,' Victoria pointed out reasonably, 'and you'll be glad of it presently, because I'll have had it, and you did say you wanted yours in three weeks' time...'

Sister Crow took no notice of this. 'I shall have that staff nurse again, I suppose—just as we were getting back into our old ways.'

She looked so harassed that Victoria found herself apologising for being so inconsiderate, and Sister Crow, never one to give up easily, pounced quickly with: 'Perhaps you will change your mind, Staff Nurse, now that you see how inconvenient it will be.'

Any nurse going on holiday or days off on Sister Crow's ward was inconvenient. Victoria said now: 'I'm sorry, Sister, but I should like my weekend. I'll go to the office about it after lunch.'

Sister Crow didn't speak to her for the rest of the day, which made it a little lonely, for Jeremy Blake, naturally enough, hadn't spoken to her either, save to issue orders to her about the patients. They were polite to each other on the ward, and once or twice when they met in the corridors he had been on the point of speaking to her, but Victoria had sailed past him with her lovely head in the air, noting as she did so that he still had a nasty bruise on the jaw where Alexander had hit him. He had spread the fiction that he had been knocked down by a swing door when the bruise first appeared, and as it was almost laughably unlikely that a doctor should knock another of his colleagues down in a hospital corridor, no one had remarked upon it, although few if any of the staff had expressed sympathy; she wasn't the only one who didn't much care for him; he had an unpleasant manner with the student nurses, especially the junior ones, who didn't like being condescended to and still less to be shouted at if they hadn't been quite quick enough to do his bidding. Victoria found herself in the unhappy position of mediator on several occasions, a fact which did nothing to improve relations between herself and Jeremy Blake. If her mind had not been so full of Alexander van Schuylen she might have been worried by it, but as it was she accepted the unpleasantness which she encountered from time to time and made the best of it.

She crossed the days off on the calendar hanging in her room, like a child impatient for Christmas, and days before Alexander was due back she washed her hair, gave herself a manicure and experimented with a new lipstick. He hadn't told her at what time he would arrive; she had an evening anyway and she would be free at five o'clock. It was halfway through the morning, while she was having coffee with Sister Crow, when that lady mentioned that an aunt was paying an unexpected visit to London. 'So I must ask you to change your off duty with mine, Staff Nurse,' she decided. 'My aunt seldom comes to town and she has booked seats at the theatre for us both. I'm looking forward to a delightful evening.'

It was on the tip of Victoria's tongue to say that she

had been looking forward to a delightful evening too, but what was the use? The poor Old Crow didn't have much fun, and in any case it was obvious that she intended to have her own way whatever Victoria said. It was a bitter blow after a whole long week of waiting, but Alexander might not get back until the evening. She hadn't heard from him, but then she hadn't expected to, nor had she expected the extravagant bouquet of flowers which had arrived halfway through the week. The card with it had merely borne his initials, but she had read it a dozen times or more, and had arranged the flowers around her room to the intense curiosity of her friends and her own great satisfaction.

Victoria didn't see Alexander's actual arrival; she was wholly occupied in persuading the irascible Major that an inhalation would be of the greatest benefit to him. A student nurse had already been routed in her efforts to get him snugly under a towel with the inhaler; she had gone in search of Victoria, snorting her indignation at the names he had called her, and had thankfully handed the task over to her. She stood beside him now, the offending inhaler in one hand, the towel in the other, calmly letting his rage wear itself out on her imperturbable front.

When he had at last rumbled to a halt, she said: 'It's no use, Major. Sir Keith ordered it and it's for your own good—besides, half the ward are having them, otherwise none of you would get a wink of sleep because of the coughing.'

He mumbled crossly: 'You're a damn bossy young woman!'

'Yes, aren't I? Now be a good boy,' she wheedled. 'I'm getting all behind with my work and it's almost eight o'clock, the night people will be on in a minute.'

She smiled at his cross old face and very reluctantly

he smiled back and allowed himself to be enwrapped in the towel. 'And mind you breathe properly,' she admonished him.

His rheumy eye peered out from the folds of the towel. It winked.

'Your boy-friend's here.' His hoarse chuckle turned into a bellowing cough so that she was obliged to pat him on the back and urge him to take deep breaths while all the time she was longing to look round and see if it really was Alexander. When she finally looked behind her, it was to see Jeremy Blake coming up the ward.

She sighed and looked pointedly at the clock over the door. Most of the medical staff obeyed the unwritten rule not to come into a ward—unless it was urgent—during the changeover from day duty to night, and night duty to day. Either Doctor Blake hadn't heard of this sensible understanding, or he didn't agree with it. She went to meet him in her usual calm manner, wished him a good evening and enquired:

'An admission? We've only one bed…'

He shook his head. 'No. I thought I'd take some blood from Mr Cox. Let me have the things, would you—and a nurse.'

'The Path Lab's closed,' she pointed out reasonably, 'and unless it's really urgent it won't be done tonight. They're on call, but only for cross-matching and so on. Besides, Mr Cox has had a wretched day and he's tired.'

'I'll decide what I wish to do on the ward, Staff Nurse. I'm not busy at the moment and it suits me to do it now.'

'In that case,' she told him without any heat, 'I must ask you to get whatever you need for yourself, and as to a nurse—they're just going off duty, as you well know, so there's no one available. I have the report to give.'

She swept down the ward and into the office, and the

night staff nurse, a girl with whom she had trained and therefore a close friend, observed:

'Whew, what's put your back up, Vicky? You look dangerous!'

Victoria took her seat at the desk and pulled the Kardex towards her. No sooner had she done so than Doctor Blake, without knocking on the door, flung it open and said nastily: 'Since I can get no co-operation from the nursing staff, I shall return tomorrow morning at eight o'clock. In the meantime I shall report you to the appropriate authorities.'

Victoria opened her mouth to make a spirited retort to this highflown speech, but remained silent, her mouth still open, for Doctor van Schuylen had appeared silently in the doorway behind the irate RMO.

'You know, I shouldn't do that, if I were you,' he advised him, his smile cold as Doctor Blake turned to face him, every bit as surprised as Victoria. 'Perhaps you don't know of the unwritten rule about upsetting the nurses' routine when they're changing duties—unless it's urgent, when I'm sure you would find them most co-operative.'

He waited placidly while the other man recovered himself. 'What infernal...it's no business of yours...'

'Er—well, yes, in a sense it is. As an honorary consultant I imagine I should do my best to uphold the rules, written and otherwise, of the hospital.' He stood aside invitingly. 'If you care to come down to the Board Room I can give you irrefutable evidence of my appointment.' He waved an arm. 'That will allow the nurses to take the report, will it not?'

Doctor Blake went with him because there didn't seem much else he could do. He wished Victoria and the night staff nurses a glacial goodnight as he went, but Doctor van Schuylen only smiled.

As their footsteps disappeared down the corridor, Victoria's companion gasped. 'Good grief,' said her friend, 'wasn't he masterly? Serve Blake right, always coming the high and mighty on the ward. What did he want?'

Victoria told her at some length, so that by the time she had given the report it was almost half past eight. She said goodnight quickly and sped down the corridor. Where would Alexander be waiting, if he were waiting at all? He hadn't said a word to her—perhaps he had gone again. She raced round the corner straight into him and would have fallen down if he hadn't put his arms around her.

'You're in a hurry,' he commented mildly. 'Don't tell me that fellow Blake's chasing you again?'

His arms felt nice, but she didn't care for his flippant tone. 'No, he's not,' she snapped. 'I'm—I'm very late…'

He kissed her, so swiftly that he had no time to appreciate it.

'Twenty minutes,' he said, 'should be ample time for you to change. I'll be waiting outside. It's too late to go dancing, but we'll go somewhere quiet and have a meal, shall we? I've some calls to make. Could I use your telephone, do you suppose?'

She was still recovering from the kiss. 'Yes, yes, of course. Will it be all right if I wear a suit or something? I mean you're not going to wear a black tie?'

He shook his head. 'Dear girl, we only have an hour or so. Come as you are if you like.'

She laughed. 'Don't be ridiculous! I'll be quick.'

Luckily none of her friends were up from supper yet and those that were off duty were out; Victoria had the corridor to herself so that she could bathe and change without hindrance. She was exactly fifteen minutes doing it and at the end of that time went downstairs, looking eye-catching in a green dress and coat which made her hair even brighter than it was, and smelling delicately of Dioressence.

Alexander was on the steps talking to Sir Keith Plummer, who, when she came through the door, smiled and said: 'Good evening, Staff Nurse—well, I won't keep you two from your evening. Enjoy yourselves.' He went into the hospital with a gentle wink at Victoria.

As they got into the car Alexander remarked: 'I suppose I shall have to get used to men winking at you, however nicely.'

Victoria settled herself into her seat. 'I never wink back,' she told him demurely.

'I'll wring your pretty neck for you if you do,' he replied cheerfully as he took the car through the hospital gates.

They went to Kettners and ate steak and kidney pie after a glass of sherry—a noble dish which they washed down with Châteauneuf du Pape, and while the doctor contented himself with cheese, Victoria did full justice to a Crême Brûlée, and while they ate they talked trivialities because Victoria felt too shy to do otherwise and her companion didn't appear to be interested in anything more personal. But presently when they were sitting over their coffee, she said, still shy: 'Thank you for the flowers, they were lovely.'

He smiled. 'Victoria, I'm catching the midnight ferry from Dover.' And when her eyes flew to her watch: 'No, dear girl, there's plenty of time yet. I didn't tell you before because I didn't want to spoil our evening.' He smiled suddenly at her and her heart warmed. 'There's such a lot to say, isn't there, and it's so hard to know where to start. Have you got your weekend?'

She told him yes, and she told him too a little of Sister Crow's annoyance about it.

'Your family know you're coming?'

'Yes, I telephoned.'

'And did you tell them about me?'

She shook her head and coloured faintly. 'Well, no—I didn't know quite what to say.'

He smiled and asked flippantly: 'What am I going to be introduced as? An old friend or a hospital colleague—or someone who met you on the cliff path?'

She was a little bewildered by his manner. 'I—I don't know. I shall introduce you as—as…I shall just introduce you.'

He smiled again, teasing her. 'I expect your family are used to you bringing men home.'

'Well, yes, I suppose so, and my sisters too—you see there are four of us.'

'And you're all very beautiful.' He looked at her with faint mockery and although he was still smiling, there wasn't a smile in his eyes. Her heart sank. The evening wasn't turning out to be nearly as wonderful as she had hoped. She spent a few seconds trying to recall if she had said anything which could have annoyed him and could think of nothing. She asked, suddenly desperate: 'Have I said something? You look,' she paused and studied his face, 'as though you've gone a long way away.'

He sat back in his chair, staring at her. 'And would you mind if I went a long way away, Victoria?'

Her heart answered before her head could reason. 'Yes, I would mind. I—I don't think I could…' She changed in mid-sentence. 'I should miss you very much.'

'You see, Vicky, I'm not being quite fair to you, am I? I've rushed you into taking a holiday you may already be regretting—there's still time to change your mind.'

'Do you want to change yours?' she asked miserably, and was relieved to see the look on his face.

'No, never that, dear girl.' He smiled at her and this

time his eyes smiled too. 'How gloomy we have become! I hadn't meant to be, but this evening, when I saw you again, it struck me that perhaps I had monopolised you more than I should have done.'

'How could you? You've been away. Are we going by train to Weymouth or will you drive?'

He followed her mood readily enough. 'Oh, drive, I think. We can leave the car at Weymouth, I suppose—I can use my friend's while we're in Guernsey. If we leave the hospital early enough we could catch the midday boat, or would you prefer to fly?'

Victoria shook her head. 'I don't like planes.' She looked at her watch. 'Shouldn't we be going? If you're going to catch your boat...'

She smiled at him brightly and after a moment's hesitation he agreed placidly and they went out to the car together, not talking much. At the hospital Alexander got out with her and walked as he had done before to the door leading to the quadrangle, but when she put her hand out to open the door he put a great hand over hers and at her questioning glance, said: 'You'll have time to think while I'm away, Victoria.'

He bent his head and kissed her gently, then opened the door for her to go through. She whispered: 'Thank you for the dinner, and have a good trip,' and slipped away without looking back. It was dark in the quadrangle and there wasn't any chance of him seeing the tears in her eyes; all the same, she didn't look back.

The days seemed endless, and Victoria, her moods alternating between the lighthearted and dreamy and the frankly despondent, found herself a prey to a variety of doubts, all of which kept her awake at night, only to evaporate with the morning, because the morning meant that she was one day nearer seeing Alexander again.

There had been flowers once more, their advent accounting for several hours of such high spirits on her part that the patients as well as her friends remarked upon them. Even the Major paused in his diatribe of the morning's news to say: 'And what's happened to you, miss? You've had the face of an undertaker's mute for the last two days and now you look like the cat that's been at the cream!'

Victoria, her mind still full of the cellophane-wrapped spring flowers the porter had just delivered, beamed at him. 'It's such a lovely day.'

He put down *The Times*, took off his glasses and looked out of the window. 'Raining,' he declared. 'You're in love, young lady.' He transferred his gaze to her face and to prevent herself from agreeing with him happily she said hastily: 'Your pills, Major,' and popped the spoon into his mouth, put a glass of water in his hands and sped on to the next patient who was far too ill to care a tinker's cuss about her.

But Sister Crow noticed, remarking tartly that Victoria looked happy enough to be going to her own wedding; so did Jeremy Blake, who, on his way round the ward later in the morning with Sister Crow, paused to examine some X-rays Victoria had fetched for him. He held them up to the light and studied them with a rather pompous air, and without taking his eyes from them remarked to the Old Crow:

'Our staff nurse is looking delighted with herself this morning, Sister. I fancy she must have good news.' His pale eyes slid sideways to glance at Victoria. 'Or perhaps flowers from the boy-friend.'

She returned his glance steadily, her pink cheeks very faintly pinker. He must have seen the flowers when the porter had brought them up to the ward or he might have been in the porter's lodge when they were delivered. She thought it unlikely that he had seen where she had hidden them—in the linen cupboard, in an old-fashioned china jug Sister, for some reason best known to herself, insisted on keeping on the ward inventory.

She didn't answer him and Sister Crow, who although stern and strict with her nurses, protected them like a mother hen with chicks from outside criticism, said:

'That will do, Doctor Blake.' She folded her arms across her trimly belted waist, the elbows aggressively cocked; she didn't hold with chat on a ward round—only Sir Keith might indulge in conversation if he had a mind to. In her opinion, anyone else doing so was merely wasting precious time.

Doctor Blake shot her an annoyed look and said in quite a different voice:

'I'll examine this man. Get him ready, Sister.'

The elbows became a thought more aggressive. 'If you wish to examine Mr Gibbs, Doctor, I will send a nurse to get him ready. There are none available at the moment—it is their coffee break, so you will have to wait.' Her tone implied that as far as she was concerned, he could wait for ever. 'In the meantime, perhaps you will write up Mr Bates for his Dactil—he's still very uncomfortable.'

He really had no choice. Sister Crow, to give her her due, had had years of experience in managing house doctors—even RMOs…

Victoria took her flowers with her when she went to midday dinner, going first to her room to put them lovingly in her washbasin until she was free that evening to arrange them. After dinner she went as usual over to the Home for a quick cup of tea before going back on the ward. Kitty went too, and Bunny; they stopped in the doorway of her room, staring at the bouquet overflowing the basin, and then turned on Victoria.

'Vicky, it's Doctor van Schuylen again, isn't it? He sent you the last lot—I do believe he fancies you.' It was Bunny who spoke, following Victoria out of the room again to fill the kettle at the pantry sink and put it on the gas ring. 'Is he coming back?'

Victoria turned the gas ring up high, opened the tiny fridge and got out the milk. 'Yes, he's coming back.'

'And you've got a long weekend,' persisted Bunny. 'Are you going away together? Where to?'

Tilly had joined them. 'Leave Vicky alone,' she ordered. 'She'll tell us when she wants to, if she wants to.'

She turned off the gas and made the tea and they all walked back to Victoria's room. It wasn't until they were sitting with their shoes off on the bed that Victoria told them.

'Well, I wasn't going to say anything, and you're not to blab—and it's not a bit exciting really. I'm going home for the weekend and he's got friends on Guernsey, so he's offered me a lift there and back.'

'Oh, Vicky,' sighed Bunny, who was sentimental by nature, 'how romantic! I expect you'll go for long walks in the moonlight and he'll propose.'

'Stuff,' said Victoria, who secretly hoped that he would do just that. 'It's just that we're both going at the same time.'

Her two friends looked at her and forbore from comment. 'Where is he now?' Tilly wanted to know.

'In Holland—he's got a practice there.'

'He gets around, doesn't he? He's something or other here too, isn't he? and in great demand at these different seminars.' She sighed. 'I bet they have a lovely time, they meet in such interesting places.'

'I don't know,' replied Victoria, 'I haven't asked him, I don't know much about him.'

Tilly put the mugs tidily on the dressing table, ready to wash up later.

'Time enough for that,' she said comfortably. 'What about the two o'clock medicine round in the meantime?'

It was during that night that Victoria had a dream, far too vivid, in which she knew, in some unexplained, dreamlike way, that Alexander had girl-friends all over the world and sent them flowers too. She woke convinced that this was true because the dream had seemed so real, and spent the day in such low spirits that Sister Crow advised her to get herself a tonic and her friends, sympathetic and carefully nonchalant as well as quite unaware of the cause of her long face, bore her off to the cinema, then crowded into her room afterwards eating the fish and chips someone had had the forethought to buy, and drinking vast quantities of tea. It was late by the time they had washed up the last mug and taken turns for the bathrooms and Victoria, when she got into bed, slept at once and all night so that when she wakened the next morning she wondered if perhaps the dream had only been a dream after all. She wasted so much time lying in bed thinking about it that she had to rush into her uniform and go down late to breakfast where, buttering bread thickly and gulping down tea, she forgot all about it in the early morning rush to get on duty in time.

She had another evening that day. It was when she was going off duty, a little late because the part-time staff nurse who covered the ward for Sister and her days off had been delayed. Not that it mattered; she had nothing much to do, there was no point in packing the few things she would need for at least two days. She was halfway down the stairs when Jeremy Blake caught up with her and slowed his pace to suit hers.

'I owe you an apology,' he started, and Victoria stared

at him in astonishment. 'I'm sorry for my rudeness—perhaps we could cry quits?'

She looked at him as they reached the landing leading to the surgical wards. He was half smiling, but his eyes were cold and she wondered why he should bother to apologise when it was so obvious that his heart wasn't in it. All the same, it would be much easier on the ward if they maintained some semblance of friendship.

'All right,' she said, 'I'll accept your apology. It's much easier to work with people if you're on good terms with them, isn't it?'

She gave him a little nod and ran down the stairs to the ground floor, and on the way over to the Home tried to decide why he had bothered to seek her out and why he wanted to get on good terms with her again. For no reason she could think of, and certainly no good reason. She shrugged the little incident off and went along to the sitting room to join her friends at a belated and ample tea, and was caught up at once in the never-ending shop talk. She usually disliked it, but now she welcomed it as a distraction from her own thoughts.

Victoria was off at eight o'clock the day before her weekend was to begin. She had spent her off-duty putting her night things into a case, washing her hair and doing her nails, although she didn't even know at what time Alexander was to fetch her in the morning—come to that, she didn't even know if he was back in England. She decided on an early night and went to bed rather cross; probably he had forgotten all about her. She remembered her dream and, a prey to a variety of wild thoughts, went immediately to sleep, to be awakened ten minutes later by Nurse Black.

'There's a call for you.' Beauty was shaking her shoulder urgently and breathing heavily because she had had to run up two flights of stairs. 'I was going through the hall and the telephone rang. I answered it and it's for you, Staff.'

Victoria yawned hugely. 'Oh, no—did they say who they were?' She was bemused by her ten minutes' oblivion and snuggled her head back on to the pillow again as she spoke, her eyes already shut.

Beauty sounded almost despairing, 'Oh, Staff, do wake up! I don't know who it is, only he said to tell you that if you keep him waiting too long he'll miss the boat. I think,' she essayed belatedly, 'it's that Dutch doctor.'

She jumped a little as Victoria surged out of bed, dragged on her dressing gown, thrust her feet into her slippers and in a state of great disarray, tore out of the room. Little Nurse Black, who liked Victoria very much, tidied her bed for her before she followed more sedately, shutting the door gently behind her.

'Dear girl,' said Alexander's voice in Victoria's now wideawake ear, 'were you fast asleep? A little early, surely?'

How disconcerting the man was, never saying Hullo or How are you, so that she might have time to shake her addled, happy wits together!

'I didn't know what time—I thought I'd better be ready. I was tired,' she finished snappily.

'But not cross. I'll be outside the Home at nine o'clock. Snatch some breakfast before then, we want to get the one o'clock boat from Weymouth.'

She nodded, just as though he were there, beside her. 'I'll be ready.'

'Now go back to bed and go to sleep. Goodnight, Victoria.'

She said softly, 'Goodnight, Alexander,' and listened while he hung up and the line went dead, then went slowly upstairs again to do exactly as he had bidden her; get into her bed and go to sleep.

Victoria was up, dressed, breakfasted and seething with impatience long before nine o'clock. She sat on the end of her bed watching the hands of her wrist watch crawl round its face, and when at last they were on the hour she forced herself to go on sitting for another two minutes in case he should find her too eager. She was wearing the cinnamon outfit again; she darted to the mirror just once more to peer at her reflection and then, stamping down a strong desire to do her hair just once more too, went down to the front door. The Mercedes was outside and Alexander was sitting behind the wheel, leaning back comfortably, smoking his pipe. He looked disappointingly placid, and if she had hoped that his expression would alter when he turned his head and saw her, she was doomed to disappointment. He got out of the car, looking pleased to see her and no more than that, said Hullo and put her case in the boot. But when she was in the car, sitting beside him, he turned to look at her with a face which was still placid, but his eyes made up for the vague, let-down feeling she had felt, and as though he had guessed her thoughts he said on a laugh: 'We couldn't have chosen a more public spot to meet, could we?' He waved his hand, and following its sweep, Victoria was forced to agree with him. The theatre staff, idle for a few minutes before the day's list started, were at a window, so was Home Sister from her little office in the Home, and through the open door leading into the hospital, a constant stream of nurses on their way to the first coffee break paused to stare. Victoria shuddered delicately; she could guess the conversation over the coffee cups, by the time she got back in three days' time, they would have forgotten all about her going away with the Dutch doctor, but at the moment she provided a nice morsel of gossip to help along the usual stodge of ward news.

'A pity,' said her companion thoughtfully, 'that we haven't the time to give them value for their money.'

Victoria stopped fiddling with her seat belt in order to look at him. The gleam in his eyes which she had already so happily noticed had become more pronounced; she decided that it would be wiser not to ask him just what he meant; instead she told him meekly that she was ready when he was, and was rewarded by his laugh.

They talked the whole time on the journey to Weymouth, but never once about themselves. Over the coffee they stopped to drink, he spoke vaguely about his work and his family, discussed his dogs, described his elderly housekeeper and had so little to say about himself that Victoria was left with the feeling that she knew nothing about him, a state of affairs which she recognised as unsatisfactory, and all the more so because she was so besotted by him that it didn't really matter in the least.

They made excellent time; there was still more than an hour before the boat sailed. They slid smoothly along the wide curve of Weymouth's seafront, pleasantly empty so early in the year although the April sun was bright if not very warm. Halfway along it, Alexander turned off into the town, garaged the car, transferring Victoria and the cases into a taxi. On board he installed her in the half-empty ship and disappeared, to reappear five minutes later with the news that he had a table for lunch; news which pleased her very much, because she had breakfasted early and sketchily.

There were a few people in the restaurant; they lunched at leisure so that they were well out to sea by the time they had finished, and because the sun was still shining and the air smelled fresh after London, Victoria elected to fetch a scarf for her hair and they went up on deck, where they walked up and down and round and round, occasionally leaning over the side to watch the sea below. Mostly they talked and when, occasionally, they fell silent, Victoria, hanging over the side of the boat, her elbow touching his, was happy because although they weren't saying a word, it was as though they were talking all the time…

She peered sideways at him and found him watching her, and her cheeks already pink from the wind, took on a more vivid colour. His eyebrows arched and his mouth curved in a smile and she looked away, only to turn to him again when he said gently:

'For such a pretty girl, Victoria, you're shy.' He flung an arm round her shoulders. 'Think of me as a friend, dear girl,' he advised her. And then, lightly, 'Tell me, how is our Doctor Blake?'

It was impossible advice he had given her, but it was a relief to have something else to talk about. She told him about the apology at some length. 'It's as though he wants to be friendly,' she explained, 'and that's a good thing, because we have to see each other every day and it was a little difficult.'

'Yes,' Alexander turned to study her. 'You're such a nice person yourself, you don't always see the nastiness in anyone else, do you? Let's hope he means it.'

'Why ever shouldn't he?' she wanted to know.

He didn't answer her, but looked at his watch. 'Time for tea,' he suggested cheerfully.

They had barely finished the meal when the Casquettes lighthouse came into sight and then distant Alderney, and presently, ahead of them, Guernsey and the little islands wreathing its harbour. They made no haste to go ashore when the boat docked; it was as quick to go last as first, Alexander declared. Victoria, who disliked crowds, was content to lean over the rail and presently saw her parents and waved happily. 'Is anyone coming to meet you?' she asked.

'Yes—they're a little to the left of your people. I hope I'm to meet your three sisters.'

'Of course. Let's go now, there's almost no one left.'

Her family fell upon her lovingly, as though it had been years instead of weeks since she had last seen them. She embraced and was embraced and finally said: 'This is Doctor van Schuylen—Alexander, who was so kind as to bring me over.'

There was a round of handshaking before he said: 'My friends are here too—may I introduce them?'

There was more handshaking and a good deal of friendly talk, for Jacques, his friend, was the son of an acquaintance of Mr Parsons, and his wife Prue remembered meeting Amabel on the tennis courts last summer. It was all very jolly and gay, and Victoria had a small stabbing doubt that perhaps now that Alexander was with his friends he might not want to spend his days with her—a doubt most agreeably squashed when he told her for everyone to hear who chose: 'I'm coming for you tomorrow morning—is nine o'clock too early? We'll have the whole day.'

He smiled nicely at her and her heart jumped absurdly. She pushed her hair out of her eyes impatiently and said softly: 'That will be lovely,' and watched the little sparks in his eyes as he looked at her.

'Yes, it will be lovely,' he said.

CHAPTER FOUR

THERE was a fierce wind blowing when Victoria got up the next morning, although the sun shone fitfully between scudding clouds. She crept along to the bathroom, put on slacks and a sweater and was tying back her copper hair with a velvet ribbon when Amabel came in.

'You're up early,' she remarked. 'What time is he coming?'

'Nine—I'm going down to get tea, do you want a cup?'

Her sister got on to the bed and pulled the eiderdown round her. 'Yes, please. Vicky, before the others come in—are you in love with him?'

Victoria turned to survey her sister—she and Amabel got on well together, but then Amabel got on well with most people. 'Yes,' she said at length, 'I think I am, but I have to be sure, don't I?' She gave her hair a final, rather vicious tug. 'And I don't know about him—he's quiet; I'm never quite sure what he's thinking.'

'I daresay he's had a lot of girl-friends. How old is he? Thirty-five? Well, it stands to reason...but he's nice. Do you think he likes us?'

'He thinks you're lovely, all of you—he said so.' Victoria frowned a little, remembering. 'He wanted to know why I was quite different.'

'Yes, well, it is funny, isn't it? You're so much smaller and there's your hair and you're almost thin. And look at us, great creatures, all curves and lamppost high—no wonder when we're talked about you're always called the other one.'

Victoria smiled. Being the other one was a long-standing joke in the family. 'Stay there, I'm going down to the kitchen.'

She padded through the still silent house and into the comfortable, cluttered kitchen. Mrs Dupres, the daily help, would be in later on to restore order and tidy up. Victoria put the kettle on, washed up the cups and saucers from the evening before and fetched an enormous teapot from the dresser. It was nice to be home again; she had enjoyed the previous evening, sitting around with the family, talking about hospital and making them laugh about poor old Sister Crow and telling them, rather cautiously, a little about Alexander. Not that she was able to tell them much, for she didn't know much herself, but at least she had been able to satisfy her mother's curiosity about where he lived and what he did and who his father was and how old he was.

Her mother had said: 'He looks a very nice man—rather quiet, but I fancy if he were roused he could display a fine temper.' And Victoria, remembering that time when he had knocked Jeremy Blake down with hardly a word and almost goodhumouredly, said she didn't know about that but probably her mother was right, and got up to let in Mabel and George, the family cats, whose advent obligingly provided another topic of conversation.

Her father, a quiet man by nature and more so by virtue of the women milling around the house, had said almost nothing at all, only on their way to bed he had paused on the stairs so that she could catch up with him and had said: 'I like your young man, or whatever the modern equivalent is these days, Vicky. He's got a straight eye.'

The kettle boiled and she made the tea, loaded a tray with cups and saucers, laid a smaller tray ready for her father to fetch later, and went back upstairs. As she had expected, all three sisters were now in her room. Louise was sharing the eiderdown with Amabel, but Stephanie had got right into bed. She moved over as Victoria went in and patted the space beside her. 'Here you are, Vicky—now come and tell us all about him.'

Victoria poured tea for everyone, opened the tin of biscuits she had found in a kitchen cupboard and asked with composure: 'Who?'

Louise sipped tea. 'Don't tease, we're all dying to hear about him. I think he's the handsomest man I've ever seen. Father says he'll have him in for dinner and I shall wear that new dress I bought last week, the one with the embroidery round the hem.'

Stephanie gave her sister a little push. 'Oh, don't be so silly, Louise, he wouldn't notice you if you were in cloth of gold. He's only got eyes for Vicky.'

'Nonsense,' said her eldest sister briskly, 'and anyway, as far as I'm concerned he can look his fill at the lot of you.' Which wasn't in the least true.

She had breakfast almost ready by the time her mother, dressed for the day and not a hair out of place, came downstairs. They had the meal all of them together, laughing and talking and occasionally quarrelling a little until their mother begged for a little peace while she puzzled over the meals for the day. 'Chicken,' she ruminated, 'no—a nice piece of beef—and then there's lunch.' She looked across the table at her eldest daughter. 'Will you be in, darling, or is your young man taking you out all day?'

'Mother,' Victoria was laughing and protesting too, 'he's not my young man, and I don't know.'

'I shall ask him,' her mother decided, and was howled down by all four girls. 'Mother, you can't—it's like tell-

ing him he's got to take her out to lunch! Why don't
you ask him here? or give them a picnic?'

Their mother brightened. 'I hadn't thought of that.
Vicky...?'

But Vicky, who had heard the bell peal just once, was
already on her way to the front door. She had meant to
take her time in answering it and greet him with a cool
friendliness which would give away nothing of her real
feelings; instead she flung the door wide and said joy-
ously: 'Hullo, come in—we're a bit late, but I shan't be
a minute.'

He was wearing slacks and a sweater too and anyone
less like the elegant successful doctor he was would have
been hard to find. He came inside and shut the door
behind him and said: 'Hullo, Vicky,' and kissed her so
quickly and lightly that she wasn't quite sure if he had.
'That's better,' he said composedly, 'it seems a long
time since yesterday.'

She had no answer to this; only a secret, fervent agreement she had no intention of voicing out loud, but led
him into the dining room where the family still sat. They
were grouped around the table, her three beautiful sisters
and her equally striking mother and father; she wished
with all her heart that she could have been tall and fair
like the rest of them, so that no man could fail to be
stunned by her good looks.

But apparently Alexander could. He wished them a
good morning politely, but showed no signs of being
stunned, nor of being bowled over by the battery of blue
eyes focused upon him. He declined coffee with firm
politeness and when Mr Parsons observed: 'I expect you
two want to get off, the island's lovely at this time of
year,' he replied with courteous brevity, 'Yes, we
should.'

Victoria's father glanced at her. 'Take a wind-cheater,

Victoria,' he advised, 'even if you intend to walk. It's chilly still and the forecast is for rain.'

'Yes, Father,' said Victoria, grateful to him for speeding them on their way, 'I'll get one.'

She flew upstairs and because she couldn't find hers, took Amabel's instead. It was much too large, but she didn't care. She got downstairs in time to hear Alexander say: 'About half past six, then, Mrs Parsons. I've got a picnic in the car, but if it's too cold or wet we can get lunch out.'

She caught her mother's eye and received a faint shake of the head. So her mother hadn't asked—thank heaven for that! She gave her parents each a grateful kiss for different reasons, waved to her sisters and went outside with Alexander to where the Mini he had borrowed waited.

They seemed very close to each other in the little car, but then he was such a large man. He sent it down Havelet with the speed of a terrier after a rat and at the bottom turned away from the town, along Fort Road towards St Martins, turning once more presently to dawdle along a narrower road nearer the coast.

'Pleinmont, I thought,' he gave her a sideways smile. 'Do you feel like a walk?'

Victoria nodded. 'We went there when I was home a few weeks ago. I love it—it'll be windy.'

She was right. The wind caught at them as they got out of the car and started along the cliff path, so that her hair streamed like a fiery banner around her head. The path was narrow and Alexander went in front, turning to give her a hand where he thought it needful, and she accepted it meekly, not telling him that she had walked the selfsame path since she could toddle and knew every inch of it. They paused presently, to gaze out to sea and watch the waves breaking on the rocks below.

'Nice.' Alexander's voice was contented; he took her arm and went on: 'If the wind lessens how about taking the boat over to Alderney tomorrow?'

'Lovely—your friends won't mind? Or will they come too?'

'Not tomorrow. Do you know Alderney well?'

'Yes, though I haven't been for a year or so.' She put an impatient hand up to her hair and then let it fall at his quiet: 'No, let it be, I like it like that.'

She darted a look at him. 'Just us?'

'Just us,' he smiled, and her heart beat faster; she voiced, idiotically, the thought which was uppermost in her mind. 'We haven't known each other long.'

He seemed to know what she meant. 'No. I am an impatient man, Victoria, but for the first time in my life I am prepared to be patient.'

He pulled her close and kissed her cheek; the kiss was somehow reassuring and gentle, just as his touch had been, and yet it somehow gave promise of other kisses to come. Victoria stared up at him, her eyes alight with happiness, longing to put that happiness into words and unable to do so, aware too that there was no need to do so. He laughed a little, caught her by the arm and they went on together; presently he began to tell her about his home and the busy life he led in Holland.

They stopped for coffee at Portelet and walked again, this time along the sandy shore among the rocks, and only turned back unwillingly when the rain which had been threatening began to fall in earnest. Victoria was surprised to find that Alexander knew the island almost as well as she did herself; he tooled the car along the narrow lanes, weaving his way round the coastline until finally he turned towards St Peter Port once more.

'We can't picnic,' he stated decisively. 'We'll go to

La Fregate and have lunch and see what the weather's like afterwards.'

Because of the bad weather and the earliness of the season, the restaurant wasn't full; they had a table by the window and ate grilled lobster tails, followed by spring chicken and salad and lastly Crêpes Soufflés au Citron. They drank a white burgundy and Victoria talked a great deal—and it wasn't only because of the wine; her companion had some quality which invited confidences; she found herself telling him things which she had never told before, not even to her sisters, and he listened gravely and when she demanded an answer or an explanation or criticism, gave them with a mild undemanding wisdom.

They were drinking their coffee when she stopped suddenly. 'I talk too much—I must have bored you.'

He answered her seriously. 'No, that would not be possible, dear girl. I want to know everything there is to know about you.'

'Oh, do you? I—I want to know about you too.' She blushed a little as she said it, but met his searching eyes with her own honest ones, and he leaned forward across the table and took one of her hands in his.

'And so you shall, my darling. Some of it may shock you, no doubt, but I don't believe in a marriage which isn't honest.'

Victoria was unable to take her eyes away from his. Her thoughts raced round inside her head like mad things; he had called her his darling which could mean nothing at all—it was after all, a form of address used every hour of the day by people who had no feeling at all for each other—on the other hand, it could mean all the world. And marriage—what had he said about that? She felt bewildered and probably looked it too, for he said, 'I'm going too fast, aren't I?' and let go of her hand, giving her a warm smile as he did so. His voice was gay when he asked:

'How about going over to Herm—the rain's stopped.'

It began to rain again on their way across the short stretch of water between the two islands, but they sat uncaring with the helmsman while he and Alexander discussed winds and tides and the pleasures of sailing. Herm seemed deserted when they landed; they told the boatman they would catch the last afternoon boat back and strolled off in the direction of the small group of shops close to the landing stage, to find them unexpectedly crowded with people anxious to come in out of the rain, so they followed the path instead, past the row of cottages and the pub, to the end of the tiny island, and then cut across the springy turf towards Shell Beach, very wet by now, but quite unheeding of it, they walked arm-in-arm while Alexander told Victoria about life in Holland.

When they reached the shore again they pottered about, looking for shells, until, battered by the great wind, Alexander suggested tea at the hotel. They went back across the centre of the island, past the fortified farmhouse with its tiny chapel, and went inside, although they both knew it well from past visits; outside once more, in the little garden before its door, Victoria murmured, thinking out loud: 'It's so peaceful, isn't it?' and smiled up at her companion, who didn't answer her but took her in his arms and kissed her hard on her mouth, an action which gave her a thrill of delight and pleasure and left her bewildered by its violence. She uttered a weak 'Oh', and he smiled, still without saying anything, and after a moment she smiled too because there was really no need for words between them.

Tea was rather hurried, for they had been dilatory on their way to the hotel and there was no other boat if they should miss the one they had planned to catch. It was the same man at the helm; they sat, one each side of him, not minding the continuing rain at all, discussing their chances of a fine day on the morrow.

Alexander had parked the Mini on the Esplanade. As they got in Victoria said: 'Mother will want you to come in for a drink.'

He flipped the car into gear and sent it along the road and round the corner and up the hill towards her home. 'I should like that,' he sounded very relaxed, 'if your mother won't object to my sodden appearance.'

'I'm wet too—look at me,' invited Victoria.

'A tempting invitation, but not on this hill, my girl.' He swung the car through the gates leading to her home and drew up before the door, which was flung open with such promptitude that she was forced to the conclusion that someone had been on the look out for them. It was Stephanie who welcomed them and Mrs Parsons' voice, very clear and compelling from the sitting room, bade them go straight in and never mind what they looked like. Everyone was home—the room, lighted by a bright fire and a couple of table lamps, looked homelike and welcoming and Mr Parsons was already on his feet, pouring sherry. He received Victoria's kiss with fatherly fondness and said over his shoulder:

'Perhaps you would prefer whisky, Alexander? I may call you that?'

'Please do, sir, and yes, whisky, I think.' He went to sit with Mrs Parsons and Victoria settled by her father, while her sisters sat together on the sofa, making a breathtakingly beautiful trio, engrossed in their visitor. Only Louise found time to say in a loud whisper:

'Vicky, you look like a half-drowned witch,' and it was unfortunate that she chose to speak at a moment when there was a momentary lull in the talk so that everybody heard it and Alexander looked across the room at Victoria, his eyes dancing. 'Yes—it's rather becoming, isn't it? We seem to have a habit of being out in the rain together.' He smiled at her, including her in his world with an air of her already being a part of it, anyway, so that her heart sang. 'We thought we might go to Alderney tomorrow, though they don't seem to think much of the weather—we can decide in the morning.' He hadn't taken his eyes off Victoria's face; now he lifted enquiring eyebrows and she nodded happily. 'Shall we use the *Sea King*?' she wanted to know. 'Isn't it a bit big for two of us to handle?'

He shook his head. 'No, not a bit of it, she's a marvellous boat and easy…!' His remark started off a lively discussion about sailing and he didn't get up to go for half an hour or more, and then reluctantly.

Stephanie got up with him. 'I'll see you out,' she declared, and Victoria who had been on the point of doing just that, was forced to wish him a cool goodbye from her chair, annoyed to see that he didn't seem in the least put out because it was Stephanie and not herself who was to see him off the premises. He turned back at the door for a final look and she scowled at him.

Stephanie came dancing back within a minute. She was, thought Victoria, eyeing her little sister smoulderingly, becoming a very pretty girl indeed. By the time she was twenty she would put the rest of them in the shade.

Stephanie met her gaze with a disarming one of her own. 'You didn't mind, did you, Vicky? You said this morning that he wasn't yours…'

'That will do, Stephanie,' remarked her mother repressively, 'and another time remember it's for Victoria to take Alexander to the door—he was her guest.'

Stephanie made a face. 'Oh, well—I just wanted to

see what he was like, really like, without everyone else there.' She shrugged her shoulders. 'He wasn't any different.'

From behind his paper her father's voice came dryly. 'Naturally not, my dear. When you're a little older you will discover that men are only different with—er—certain people.'

'Girl-friends?' enquired his daughter.

'Possibly—supposing you wait and find out for yourself?'

Stephanie went and sat down by the fire. 'Well, anyway, he's the nicest man I've ever met and terribly good-looking. He sends me!'

Her father snorted. 'The appalling language which I am forced to listen to from you young women! Now go and tell Mrs Dupres that we're ready for dinner, or I shall send you myself.' A remark which caused all four of his daughters to burst into laughter and declare him to be a dear old-fashioned creature.

Victoria woke during the night and lay listening to the wind sighing around the trees in the garden and the rain lashing the window. There would be no Alderney in the morning, she thought sleepily; they would have to think of something else. She was almost asleep again when she decided to take Alexander to visit Uncle Gardener.

The weather was, if anything, a little worse when she got up. Perhaps Alexander wouldn't come that morning because of it. She went down and got the tea again because no one else seemed to be about, but when she got back to her room, it was to find her sisters crowded on her bed. She wished them good morning a little tartly and pointed out that it hadn't been her turn to get the tea, but she was interrupted before she had half finished.

'Now do tell us, Vicky, we want to know,' demanded

Louise, 'does he fancy you? Are you going to get married?'

Victoria drank tea with maddening slowness. 'If you mean Alexander, I have no idea to both questions. He— I told you, he just happened to be coming here for the weekend and it happened to be the one I had asked for...'

'Liar,' said Stephanie succinctly. 'I saw the way you looked yesterday when I went with him to the door...you're crazy about him.' She added, unusually gentle. 'If I'd known, Vicky, I wouldn't have teased you.'

Victoria smiled at her. 'No, love, I know you wouldn't, only don't ask me any questions yet—I don't know myself.'

Amabel said in her gentle way: 'You're going out again today.'

'Well, we can't go sailing, can we? I thought we might go and see Uncle Gardener.'

Victoria had spoken lightly, hoping with all her heart that he would come that morning and still not quite sure that he would. Breakfast seemed to take an unnecessarily long time; she had finished long before anyone else and engrossed herself in the morning's paper, reading not a word of it while her ears strained for the sound of the door bell, and her family, with fond sympathy, listened with her even though they were all talking at once as they usually did. When the bell did at last go, she put the paper down with a slowness which didn't deceive those around her, saying: 'I'll go, shall I, since I've finished,' and slipped from the room.

He was very wet, although he seemed unaware of it. He cast off his rainproof jacket as he came in, caught her close and kissed her, so that rain or no rain, the world became a perfect place on the instant.

'Come walking, dear girl?' he asked. She moved a little way away from him because she had the absurd idea that if she stayed near to him he would hear the thudding of her heart against her ribs.

'Yes, of course, but I wondered if you would like to come to Castle Cornet with me—the curator is an old friend of my father's and we've known him all our lives. I usually go and see him when I'm home.' She started for the stairs. 'Everyone's in the dining room if you like to go in.'

She was back within minutes, well wrapped against the weather, to find Alexander standing chatting to her father, seemingly oblivious of the eyes focused upon him, but once outside, walking beside her up Havelet to Hauteville, he made the remark that not only were her three sisters remarkable in their looks; their stares were even more devastating.

Victoria laughed. 'They're only curious about you,' she defended them. 'Did I hear Mother asking you back for drinks?'

He gave her a sidelong glance from his blue eyes. 'Yes—she asked me for dinner too.'

She met his eyes and smiled a little. 'That'll be nice.' They were going down the steps from Hauteville, leading them towards the Market, and he caught her hand because they were steep and slippery, but at the bottom she withdrew it gently and walked on beside him, looking sedate.

Uncle Gardener was delighted to see them. Despite the awful weather they found him on the ramparts, lovingly tending his flowers, and when Victoria introduced Alexander, he said, 'Ah, yes—the young man in the yacht, isn't it? We watched you…' He shot a mischievous glance at Victoria, who frowned at him repressively. 'We were interested in the boat—a nice thing.'

The two men started an easy, casual conversation about sailing and she strolled away, poking at the flowers and leaning over the ramparts to watch the sea boiling below. Presently they joined her. 'Magnificent, isn't it?' asked Uncle Gardener. 'Very exhilarating, but bad for my flowers. Are you much of a gardener, Doctor van Schuylen?'

The three of them leaned against the old stone wall, happily discussing bulbs and their treatment and becoming drenched with the rain. Neither of the men took any notice of the weather at all and Victoria, already wet, her hair plastered to her head under her scarf, was perfectly happy to stand between them listening, although when Mr Givaude suggested coffee she was glad to follow him through the familiar Prisoners' Walk and round the corner to his house, where she threw off her wet things and went to the kitchen where Mrs Watts, the housekeeper, was making the coffee. She made shift to dry her hair by the fire and as it was hopeless to put it up she borrowed a shoelace from the accommodating Mrs Watts and tied her still damp hair back and went to join the men.

They were poring over charts, of which Uncle Gardener had a great many, but they got up politely when she went in, to return to them with obvious relief when she said: 'Don't stop whatever it is you're doing, I'm going to sit by the fire and get my feet dry.' She poured their coffee and carried it over to the table where they were sitting, together with some of Mrs Watts' splendid cake, and then went back to drink her own and toast her stockinged feet by the fire's warmth. The two men drank their coffee absentmindedly and she refilled their cups without asking them, for they were so deeply engrossed that she doubted if they would have heard her anyway. She demolished two slices of cake, drank her second cup of coffee and lulled by the quiet voices of the men and the peace of the little room, closed her eyes, to open them presently upon Alexander's smiling face and Uncle Gardener's slightly puzzled one.

'Bless my soul,' said that gentleman, 'you've been to sleep, child. Do you feel all right?'

Victoria sat up. 'Yes, of course, Uncle. It was so warm and pleasant I nodded off.' She looked enquiringly at Alexander to see if he was ready to go, but Mr Givaude intercepted the glance and said diffidently:

'Vicky, I wondered if you would like to stay to lunch, the two of you. There's bound to be plenty and the truth is, Alexander and I are having a most interesting discussion.'

She smiled at his serious face. 'I'd love to,' she said promptly, 'that is if Alexander hasn't anything else...?'

She stole a quick glance at the doctor as she spoke and was reassured by his face. She picked up the coffee cups, stacked them neatly on the tray and said: 'I'm going to see if there's anything I can do for Mrs Watts while you finish your talk.' She made for the door and Alexander went to open it for her, the smile on his face such that she all but danced to the kitchen.

Over lunch Uncle Gardener wanted to know when they were returning.

'Tomorrow,' Victoria told him. 'It was only a weekend, you know.' She didn't say any more, but pressed him to some more of his own rhubarb pie, hoping that he wouldn't comment on her reasons for coming home again when she had only just returned from a week's holiday. He passed his plate for some more pie and addressed the doctor instead.

'Of course you naturally wanted to meet Vicky's parents,' he observed, a remark which caused her to colour up delightfully—it made Alexander sound as though he were on trial; she hoped that he didn't feel as embarrassed as she did. It seemed he didn't.

'That's right,' he agreed calmly, 'that was my main reason for coming. I shall be rather tied up with work when I get back.' He caught Victoria's eyes. 'I had other reasons for coming too,' he added, and she had the impression that this time he was speaking to her.

They went to the cinema in the afternoon, and sat, her hand in his, watching a mighty Hollywood epic which afterwards Victoria couldn't remember anything of, although her memory played no tricks when it came to remembering the feel of Alexander's hand, large and gentle, holding hers.

They walked home arm in arm along the Esplanade with the unrelenting wind and rain buffeting them, talking about films and Uncle Gardener and their journey back the next day. At the door she asked if he would like to come in, but he shook his head, saying casually that he would be back around seven and bidding her so casual a farewell that her peace of mind was seriously disturbed.

The evening was a success, though, for the doctor was an amusing talker and a very good listener besides. Victoria, sitting beside her mother as they drank their coffee in the charming drawing room, was forced to admit that he was a very charming man and knew to a nicety just how much attention her three sisters expected, and it was obvious too that her parents liked him. She became a little silent, content to watch him covertly, and when from time to time he looked at her and smiled, she smiled happily back, feeling secure once more.

They started back the next morning with the family there to see them off. They stayed on deck watching Guernsey fading slowly into the grey seas and sky around them, and then walked the decks, undeterred by the rough wind and the boat's heaving, something which didn't impair their appetites in the least. They ate their lunch in an almost empty restaurant and then walked again until Weymouth harbour closed in on them.

The Mercedes was waiting for them on the quayside, something Victoria hadn't expected, and when she mentioned it to Alexander he looked faintly surprised, as though the possibility of having to go and fetch it for himself hadn't occurred to him. She got into the car while he paid off the garage hand who had driven it down, reflecting that he was a man who expected and obtained the best out of the material things of life while at the same time perfectly able to shift for himself should he need to. He got in beside her, eased the car away from the medley of vehicles around them and said: 'We'll stop for tea as soon as we get the other side of Dorchester, shall we? Wimborne, I should think. There's a place in Cobham where we can have dinner.'

They stopped in Wimborne as he had suggested and had their tea in a pleasant, old-fashioned hotel in the little town's square, and then drove on again, not much worried about the time, for as Victoria had explained, as long as she was on duty by half past seven in the morning nothing else mattered overmuch. All the same Alexander made good speed towards London, and it was well before eight o'clock when he slowed down in Cobham and turned into the grounds of the Fairmile Hotel. It was a pleasant country house, rather full because it was Sunday evening, but by the time she returned from seeing to her hair and face, a table had been found for them and the doctor had ordered drinks. She sat down opposite him and began diffidently: 'It's been a lovely weekend—thank you for taking me, Alexander,' and was disconcerted when he replied blandly:

'But, my dear girl, surely you know that the weekend

was planned entirely to suit my own wishes? How else was I to make your family's acquaintance?'

This remark Victoria found difficult to answer, she sipped her Dubonnet trying to look as though she had understood and failing. And it became obvious to her that he had no intention of enlightening her either, for he said with a half smile: 'I'm going over to Holland tomorrow.'

She noticed that he didn't tell her at what time, nor did he ask her if she would be free. 'I've got a lot of work to get through in the next few weeks,' he went on. 'My secretary has remorselessly filled every day for me.'

She said lightly to cover her hurt: 'She sounds a dragon, but I expect you couldn't do without her. Have you had her long?'

'Years—how quickly the days went, Victoria.'

She wasn't going to let him see how she felt. 'They always do,' her voice was still light, 'but I expect if we had too much free time we shouldn't enjoy it half so much. We're lucky at St Judd's though, once we're trained we get a long weekend every month as well as six weeks' holiday.' All of which, she thought sourly, he must already know.

'And can you leave if and when you want to?'

'Well, no, we have to give a month's notice. I suppose if there were some really good reason for going, it could be arranged. I've never had occasion to ask. Do you plan to do any sailing in Holland?'

He didn't answer at once, for a waiter came to take their order and there was the business of choosing what to eat. They were eating their iced melon when he said: 'About sailing—yes, I shall spend most weekends on the Loosdrechtsche Plassen, I expect.' And when she wanted to know where that was he explained: 'Near Utrecht. I've a little house—a cottage really, on the lakeside in

Loenen. It's delightful there in the early summer before the tourists come.'

He went on to talk about the village and the river Vecht running close by and the histories of some of the old houses lining its banks, and Victoria listened to every word, treasuring them up to remember later because he was going away and he hadn't said that he was coming back. He talked with gentle inconsequence while they ate their Aylesbury duckling, Crêpes Suzettes, and sampled the cheese board which followed, and because he didn't seem to want to talk about themselves at all, she followed his lead and became a little gay, telling him amusing stories of hospital life. It was rather an effort even though the claret they were drinking had cheered her up a little. They lingered over coffee and it was after ten when they left the hotel and once more got into the car, and because Alexander drove fast and the London streets were almost empty she found herself outside the hospital long before she wished. She had her hand on the car door ready to get out as she embarked on her thanks; a hotch-potch of lovely dinners, heavenly weekends and good trips which he sliced off abruptly by saying mildly: 'Don't chatter, girl, I'm coming in.'

He got out before she could move and opened her door for her, then walked, as they had walked before, through the hospital's entrance, past the porter in his box, along the passage to the quadrangle, to fetch up silently before the Home door, where the doctor put a purposeful hand on its handle so that she couldn't go inside.

'Will you miss me?' he asked, and Victoria frowned in the dark because he had sounded so lighthearted, as though he were sure of her answer. She longed to say no, not in the least, but her treacherous tongue answered 'Yes, of course,' before she could stop it. She wished she had curbed it when he said 'Good,' in what she considered to be an odiously placid voice. Only the beginnings of a fine temper prevented her from bursting into tears when he bent down and kissed her lightly on one cheek and said: 'Goodnight, Victoria.' He opened the door for her then, leaving her no choice but to go through. She flounced past him, quite bewildered. 'Goodnight,' she managed in a voice vibrant with emotion. She didn't look at him.

It was Sister Crow's day off and the ward was busy in a muddled sort of way. By dinner time Victoria had dealt with three admissions, an outburst of temper on the part of the Major, a nurse with toothache which necessitated her going off duty, sundry visits from physiotherapists, Path Lab staff, social workers, not to mention Johnny Dawes and Matron, who, for some reason best known to herself, stopped and spoke to every single patient on the ward. Victoria came back from her dinner cross and a little untidy with the prospect of a long afternoon before her. She flung open the office door, having sent all but one nurse to dinner, and found Alexander sitting on the side of the desk, staring out of the window and whistling cheerfully. Delight at seeing him again when she had spent most of the night telling herself that he had disappeared for ever out of her life mingled strongly with an uprush of rage because she wasn't looking her best and because all the awful things she had been thinking about him were probably not true after all. She crashed the door to with a fine disregard for the notice on it requesting quiet at all times, and said loudly: 'Well, what a surprise!'

Alexander had got off the desk to lean against it, his hands in his pockets, his face bland, although his blue eyes were studying her keenly.

'You're surprised,' he observed, and she saw with annoyance that he was quite unimpressed by her strong
feelings. 'I can't think why,' he went on reasonably. 'I
didn't say goodbye to you—you surely didn't think that
I would go away without doing that?'

She stayed where she was by the door, chained by
bad temper. 'You didn't say you were going to...'

He smiled then and stood up straight, towering over
her in the small room. 'I have to go,' he said, 'and perhaps it's a good thing, for I see that you are in no mood
to while away an idle moment. Had a bad morning?' He
grinned suddenly. 'Your hair's coming down,' he observed cheerfully. 'I won't keep you, then you'll have
time to do something to it before you start your afternoon.'

He had come very close to put his hands on her shoulders. 'Dear girl,' his voice was gentle and very understanding of her black mood, 'I shall come back, quite
soon, remember that.' She saw the gleam in his eyes as
he bent his head to kiss her, with most satisfying thor-
oughness, on her mouth.

He had gone before she had time to say anything. She
sat down at the desk, making no attempt to tidy herself,
going over his words several times, as though by doing
so she could make more of them. Presently she sighed
and smiled and went to the small mirror on the wall and
made shift to pin up her hair under her cap, before going
into the ward to see what the nurse there was about.

The days were empty after he had gone; even the arrival of more flowers—red roses in an overwhelming
abundance this time—did nothing to help matters. The
week toiled to its close with its admissions of new patients, its discharges of old ones; Sir Keith Plummer's
stately rounds and Johnny Dawes' harassed ones because
Doctor Blake was on holiday, and always the daily

round of medicines, treatment, injections and bedmaking, interlarded with the checking of laundry. A dull week, thought Victoria, glad to see it go, despite her pleasant day off with Uncle Gardener's sister, a widowed lady of formidable appearance and the disposition of a lamb, who lived in a severe-looking terrace house in Pimlico.

The house was as deceiving in its appearance as its owner, for once inside, it revealed a pleasant, somewhat shabby comfort, a very small, well-kept garden at the back and a semi-basement kitchen, which for all its inconvenience was extremely cosy. Martha, Mrs Johnson's household help, spent her days there, cooking delicious food which Victoria did full justice to when she visited her friend. She had spent some time there when she had gone that week, sitting on the kitchen table, sampling Martha's little cakes while she evaded the sharp questions her hostess put to her. Uncle Gardener, it seemed, had written to his sister and told her all about Alexander. Victoria had parried the questions with vague answers which she could see didn't satisfy either of her elderly listeners in the least; she was forced to bring the interrogation to a close by declaring that she was starving, a plea which served as a good red herring and forced her to eat an enormous meal which she didn't really want, because Mrs Johnson declared that she had no doubt that Victoria never had quite enough to eat in hospital, 'Although,' she added cunningly, 'I daresay that nice doctor takes you out and gives you a good meal whenever he can.'

'We went out once or twice,' admitted Victoria, spooning up Martha's delicious onion soup, 'but he's left England now, you know. I daresay we shan't see each other again.' She spoke with a careless lightheartedness which she felt sure would deceive her listeners. Mrs

Johnson's only comment was: 'That's as may be, Vicky dear,' and pressed her to a mouth-watering portion of Martha's steak and kidney pudding. Alexander wasn't mentioned for the whole of the rest of the day, but Victoria had been very conscious of his ghostly bulk in the little house.

She thought about him—when did she not?—on her way back to St Judd's that evening; he hadn't written, but she hadn't expected him to. She knew enough about members of the medical profession to realise that letter-writing came very far down on the list of their personal activities. He could have telephoned, but there again, he hadn't struck her as a man to talk trivialities into a telephone; she fancied he used that instrument as a means to an end and not for pleasure. That left little choice, in fact, only one—to return as he had said he would. But perhaps he hadn't meant what he had said. She was aware that this idea did him less than justice, but on the face of things it could be possible. Rather irritably, because she could feel a headache coming on, she decided not to think about him any more, then perhaps, in time, she might forget him.

She was mortified and disturbed to find that this undoubtedly sensible course of action wasn't as easy as she had supposed. She hadn't known that loving someone could absorb so much of her being. She struggled to obliterate him under a variety of activities; the cinema whenever her friends were free to go with her, table tennis—which she loathed—several quite unnecessary shopping expeditions to Regent Street, which had proved expensive and not very successful, and of course a stern application to work which delighted the Old Crow and badly disconcerted the nurses on the ward, for although she was a splendid worker anyway, always willing to roll up her sleeves and tackle any job which needed doing, she had begun, over the last few days, to show an alarming tendency to go around looking for work. Even the Major noticed it and reproved her in no uncertain terms. 'There's no need to go around looking for jobs, girl,' he observed testily. 'Most of the time you're run off your feet—besides, it's very disturbing.'

Victoria begged his pardon quite humbly; she had had no idea that she had been quite so zealous. She would have to watch it or she would develop into another Sister Crow. She closed her beautiful eyes for a second, visualising herself in her navy uniform and frilled cap, sitting in the office, ordering staff nurse to go and count the laundry. It seemed so improbable that she laughed and the Major rumbled. 'That's better—more like you.'

Even Johnny noticed the difference in her and asked in a brotherly fashion what was eating her. 'Not yourself, are you, old girl?' he observed. 'Nothing but frowns and thoughts far away—I might just as well not do a round.'

She turned on him. 'That's not fair! I've not forgotten anything to do with the patients, have I? Or have I?' she added weakly.

'No, ducky, nor are you likely to, only you're a bit down in the mouth, aren't you?'

Jeremy Blake, back from leave, noticed too, although his remarks weren't so kind. 'A little sour this morning, Staff,' he enquired. 'Too many late nights perhaps—oh, I forgot, it's more likely to be a lack of them, isn't it?' He smiled. 'Or am I guessing wrong?'

'Guess what you like,' said Victoria coldly, 'I couldn't care less.'

He had smiled again, a mean little smile which hardly curved his lips, and gone away, leaving her indignant.

It was Wednesday evening when the overdose came in, an hour or so before the night nurses were due on. It had been a busy day; Sister Crow had gone off duty

at five o'clock, there was a student nurse on days off
and the part-time nurse who helped out in the evenings
had telephoned to say that she couldn't come. Victoria
was left with Nurse Miller, a second-year student nurse,
and Nurse Bentley, just out of preliminary training
school, and, a timid girl by nature, still inclined to become petrified when addressed by any of her seniors.
Victoria, struggling to get the medicine round done before suppers came up to the ward, as well as innumerable
injections, felt impatience welling up within her even
while she preserved her usual calm, quiet front towards
her two helpers as well as the patients. She was dealing
with suppers when she had the message about the overdose and dispatched Nurse Miller to get a bed ready and
everything necessary for the putting up of a drip. He was
far gone, a cheerful voice informed her from the Accident Room, and although the overdose was of cannabis,
it was thought that he might have taken something else
besides, but they wouldn't know for certain until the
Path Lab had done its bit.

The patient was a well-built young man of nineteen
or so, deeply unconscious and already, Victoria was
thankful to see, on a drip. She saw him put into bed by
the porters and then went to meet Johnny as he came
through the ward doors. 'This one's a bit of a puzzle,'
he said worriedly. 'He's taken something else—probably
the hard stuff.' He glanced round the ward. 'A bit thin
on the ground, aren't you?'

Victoria explained about the part-time nurse not coming and Nurse Bentley, who had retired to the sluice,
apparently under the impression that out of sight would
be out of mind. 'You need a male nurse,' said Johnny.
'Any chance of getting one—this character might cut up
rough.'

Victoria considered. 'No—there'll be two or three on

for night duty, but Mr Cox and Mr Williams are both off. I saw them at tea.'

'Keep an eye on him, anyway, Victoria.' Johnny spoke in such a fatherly tone that she giggled and then said soberly: 'Yes, I will—and I'll ring the office and see if I can get someone else up here.' She glanced at him. 'Will you be handy if I need anything for him?'

'In the common room—and I'll pop up from time to time, but he looks pretty deep at the moment. Put him on a fifteen-minute pulse and pupil reaction, will you.'

She nodded. 'Yes—Nurse Miller can do that while Bentley gets the ward straight—thank heaven it's not visitors this evening.'

They took a final look at the boy and went back into the office, where Johnny wrote up the charts she had ready for him, and then went off, down the corridor, whistling cheerfully.

There was too much for her to do for any hope of going to supper; she sent Nurse Bentley and, when she came back, Nurse Miller. The boy was still quiet and although he was still unconscious, everything seemed satisfactory. Victoria and Nurse Bentley went round the ward, tidying the beds and making ready for the night, and presently when these chores were done, she sent the nurse to filling water jugs while she fetched the Kardex from the office and began to write it up at the boy's bedside.

She was perhaps halfway through it when Nurse Bentley came to tell her that the Major, was, as usual, being difficult about being got into bed. Victoria sighed, for she was tired and dispirited and the Major was a handful she didn't feel able to cope with. Nevertheless, she put down the Kardex, instructed Nurse Bentley to stay by the boy's bed, and walked up the ward.

The Major was determined to be nasty; it took a few

minutes of her persuasive cajoling to get him out of his
dressing gown and sitting on the side of his bed. She
had just achieved this happy state of affairs when she
heard Nurse Bentley's voice, high with fear, calling her.
The Major, to his disgust, was left where he was and
Victoria hurried down the ward. The boy was coming
to; he had an arm round poor little Bentley, whose appearance reminded Victoria forcibly of a rabbit in the
clutches of a boa-constrictor. 'Get help,' she said rapidly, unwrapping the petrified girl. 'Telephone the lodge,
say it's urgent.' She warded off a flying arm, only to be
caught up by his other hand. This, she thought bitterly,
would happen, and so much for the office and their
promise of speedy help.

The other arm came up and clamped her round the
waist and she disentangled herself with difficulty. While
she was doing it the boy opened his eyes and despite
her good sense and sound training she shuddered at their
blind, mad stare. She loosened his arm at last and said
with all the calm she could muster: 'Lie still and try to
keep quiet.' She was unprepared for the sudden lunge
he made; it brought him out of bed, and although she
was a strong girl, not easily frightened, she knew that
she would be powerless to hold him. All the same, she
warded him off and even managed to pin one arm to his
side.

'And now, back into bed,' she said with firm author-
ity. 'You're disturbing the other patients.'

He spoke then, not loudly—if he had, some of the
nearer patients, shut off by the cubicle curtains, might
have heard him and shouted for help—but in a harsh
whisper, using language which Victoria, used as she was
to the sometimes rough language from some of the men
who came into the ward, could only guess at. But whatever he was saying, it was obvious that he was in a nasty

mood. She made the mistake of slackening her hold on his arm for a split second and in the next moment he had her by the throat.

Even if she had wanted to scream—and how could she with old Mr Parker dying in the next bed?—she had no breath to do so. She gathered her strength and fought back more or less silently, sure that help was on the way.

Help had been delayed, though. Nurse Bentley, shaking with fright and aware that this was something the training school hadn't given her any lectures about, dialled the telephone with fingers which shook so much that she got the wrong number the first time, and when she did get it right, there was no answer. She stood listening to the faint burr-burr at the other end, willing someone to answer and put an end to her dilemma. Tears which she was quite unable to prevent filled her eyes and trickled down her cheeks. She was on the point of throwing the receiver on the desk, running out of the hospital and going home and never coming back again, when Doctor van Schuylen spoke from the doorway.

'Hullo, Nurse—in trouble? Can I help?'

She didn't know him from Adam, but he was a man and large and presumably a match for the patient. 'Oh, do hurry,' she gasped, 'he'll kill her!' A vague fragment of some half-forgotten lecture filtered through her muddled head—'Always give a clear and concise report whatever the circumstances, Nurse'—'Staff,' she almost wailed at him, 'in the ward—there's a drug overdose— first bed inside...'

He had gone. She picked up the receiver and in a quavering voice besought the porter who answered to send help.

Victoria fought steadily to remove her patient's hands from her throat; part of her mind told her that she had only to hold out for a very short time, but even as her mind registered this heartening fact, his grip tightened and she found herself fighting for breath. She became aware that her heartbeats sounded very loudly in her ears, her eyes ached, so did her arms. The beat changed to a steady drumming and she closed her eyes because they hurt her, then a moment later opened them again because the hands had gone from her throat, leaving her gasping for air.

'Get down on the ground, my darling,' said Alexander in a cool, no-nonsense voice, 'and breathe.'

She did as she was bid—indeed, her legs wouldn't support her any way; they folded up obligingly under her, and she lay, drawing painful little breaths, aware of the doctor's nicely polished shoes within an inch of her face and taking great comfort from them. There seemed to be a great deal of scuffling going on, but she really didn't care; just to lie and breathe was nice. Presently she became aware of more feet and then of Nurse Bentley, dripping tears on to her face and whispering: 'Oh, she's dead, she's dead!' She tried to contradict this ridiculous statement and found that not only was her throat extremely painful but that she couldn't speak, either. A funny little croak escaped her lips, but before she could try to improve upon it, she was scooped up into Alexander's arms and carried out of the ward, along the corridor and down the stairs and into the Accident Room, where he laid her carefully on one of the couches. She wanted to say 'Don't go', but the words wouldn't come; it was a relief when he took one of her hands in his and smiled down at her with such tenderness that her heart, which had steadied nicely in the past few minutes, began to thump again.

'I won't leave you, dear girl,' he assured her. 'You'll be all right presently.'

Victoria felt safe and secure. She smiled at him with something of an effort and closed her eyes. Incredibly, she dozed off.

CHAPTER FIVE

VICTORIA was aware, during the next hour or so, of things being done to her. The welcome whiff of oxygen they gave her did much to restore her, but the examination of her sore and swollen throat was something she found difficult to put up with; her eyes ached too, and her arms. She frowned faintly at Sir Keith, who to her surprise was bending over her, feeling her arms and murmuring: 'No fractures, I fancy.'

Of course there were no fractures; if she had had a voice she would have told him that she was made of good strong Parsons flesh and bone which didn't fracture easily. He examined her eyes as well and then smiled down at her, his long, thoughtful face somehow very reassuring.

'Not much damage,' he told her. 'Bed is what you need, young woman, and something for that throat.'

He turned away and she heard him muttering away to someone she couldn't see but guessed was Alexander. A moment later she heard his voice.

'You're going to be warded for a day or two, Vicky. No damage, but you're going to have a sore throat. I'll come and see you tomorrow.' He squeezed her hand reassuringly. 'Have a good sleep and don't worry.'

She stared up at his face above hers. His voice had been placid and untroubled, but his eyes were full of loving concern.

She slept badly because her throat hurt her, but towards morning, after she had managed to swallow some tea, she dropped off, to wake after an hour or two to find that her throat was a little better and that she could whisper in a hoarse croak. She tried to sit up and winced at the ache in her arms.

'Bruised,' Sick Bay Sister told her. 'Black and blue you're going to be, my girl, from your waist to your shoulders—and your neck. We've got something to help your throat—Nurse will be in presently to see to you and then we'll pretty you up a bit.'

She was as good as her word. Victoria made a sketchy breakfast of a cup of painfully swallowed Horlicks, was bathed, attired in one of her own nighties, her hair brushed and tied back, and sat up in bed. An inhalation had eased her throat, lotion had soothed her bruises and she felt almost herself. She eased herself back on her pillows and closed her eyes—a little nap would be delightful. When she opened them again Alexander was sitting by the bed, reading the *Telegraph*. There was a vase filled to overflowing with red roses on the table beside her bed and a pile of books beside it.

He put the paper down. 'Feeling better?' he wanted to know, and when Victoria whispered yes in a hoarse little voice, nodded in a satisfied way and leaned forward to take her hand in his.

'Why are you here?' she managed.

'I came to take you out to dinner,' he explained, and made it sound as though he had popped in from next door instead of crossing the North Sea. 'I had a day to spare and it's more than a week since I saw you—besides, I felt like a trip over here.'

He spoke so casually that she turned her head to look at him, and saw then that his look wasn't in the least casual. His blue eyes caught and held hers. 'My darling, don't ever let that happen again,' he said quietly. 'I have never been so afraid.' He leaned over a little further and kissed her forehead. 'Thank heaven Sir Keith was in the hospital.'

'The boy?'

'Transferred last night.'

'Poor little Bentley...'

'Yes, the child was upset, although Sister Crow told me with some asperity this morning that she's considered something of a personality by the rest of her set—I can just imagine the tale she had to tell.'

Victoria began to laugh and then stopped because it hurt too much. She waved her free hand at the roses and books. 'You? Thank you, Alexander.'

'You shall have the moon and the stars if you want them,' he assured her gravely, and she went slowly pink under his stare. He studied her at his leisure, and when the pink had faded went on more briskly: 'I telephoned your parents and told them not to worry and that there was no need for them to come to London. You'll have to go away for a few days before you go back on the ward, but we'll think about that later. Now I must go, but I'm coming back later on.'

He kissed the hand he was holding, put it tidily back on the bedcover and went away.

He was back after tea, and Victoria, who had sustained visits from Matron, the Old Crow, various of her friends and Johnny, not to mention Sir Keith—but not, to her relief, Doctor Blake—turned a weary face to the door as he came in, so that he said at once: 'You're tired—I shan't stay above a moment or so. You're longing to sleep, aren't you?'

She smiled at him. 'Yes,' she croaked, 'but I'd rather talk to you.'

Alexander stood at the foot of the bed, his face calm. 'How nice,' he said placidly, 'but not now. Listen—I met Mrs Johnson this afternoon as I was leaving the hospital—I overheard her asking for you at the porter's lodge. I had no idea that she was Mr Givaude's sister, but she so obviously knew you well that it seemed a good idea to speak to her. You're to go there and stay for a few days as soon as you're fit to leave here. She insists upon it, and she's coming to see you tomorrow.'

Victoria smiled again. 'I shall love that.' She paused and studied his quiet face. 'You're going away again, aren't you?'

He nodded. 'Yes, my darling—work, you understand. I'm a slave to it.' He came round the bed and bent to kiss her gently. 'I shall be back, Vicky, and next time I hope we can have that dinner date.'

It was three days before they allowed her to leave the hospital to go and stay with Mrs Johnson, and even then her neck was all colours of the rainbow, so that although the weather was quite warm she was forced to wear a high-necked, long-sleeved dress, and even that wasn't enough and she found it necessary to drape a scarf around her throat as well where the green and purple fingermarks were still very much in evidence. But she had got her voice back and although her throat was still sore she found it possible to talk and eat in fair comfort.

She was dressed and waiting in her room when Matron came to see her.

'Ready for Mrs Johnson, Staff Nurse?' she enquired. 'I'm glad to find that you have made such an excellent recovery. I am very sorry indeed that this has happened, and I hope a week's sick leave will put you back on your feet,' she paused and added with some delicacy, 'I hope too, that this unpleasant experience has not given you a distaste for nursing. You have a most promising future, most promising, and I should be sorry to see it jeopardised in any way.'

Victoria murmured suitably. Matron was a nice

woman, but she spoke as if there was no other future for Victoria outside nursing. She was on the point of mentioning that her future wasn't quite decided, but something stopped her; after all, Alexander might call her his darling, but there was nothing out of the ordinary in that nowadays. It was perfectly possible to be a man's darling until he met another girl who would be slightly more darling. She listened to Matron's kindly remarks and answered pleasantly when it was necessary, and was relieved when the Home maid came to tell her that Mrs Johnson was downstairs.

Mrs Johnson drove her own car, an elderly Austin Ten, almost a museum piece, but in perfect working order, which in itself was an astonishing thing, for Mrs Johnson was by no means a careful driver. They journeyed to Pimlico in a series of little rushes, sudden applications of the brake and a terrible grinding of gears, none of which seemed to worry the Austin's owner in the least, and Victoria, who had driven with her hostess before, knew better than to comment upon their eccentric progress. All the same, she was relieved when they reached the house and Martha came to open the door and hug her to an accompaniment of Well, I nevers— the villain—look at your poor neck! and suchlike consoling remarks. Victoria was drawn into the small house's comfort, made to sit in a chair in the sitting room and plied with tea, and because Martha had baked an assortment of cakes especially for her, she made a good meal, despite her sore throat.

After tea Mrs Johnson insisted upon her staying where she was. 'Martha will unpack your case,' she said comfortably. 'I'm so glad to have you here, child. A few days' rest and quiet will do you a world of good—it must have been a shocking experience.'

'Yes, it was. I—I was terrified. I couldn't believe my ears when Alexander...'

Mrs Johnson gave her a keen glance. 'A resourceful young man, I fancy, Victoria, and very dependable. I like what I saw of him, so did your Uncle Gardener.'

High praise indeed, thought Victoria. Anyone finding favour in her brother's sight was sure to be accepted by his sister without question. She asked: 'Did you have a long talk with Alexander?'

'No,' said Mrs Johnson, 'at the most ten minutes, but I took an instant liking to him. He's back in Holland, I gather?'

Victoria stared fixedly at her shoes, thinking what a long way away Holland was. 'Yes,' she said at length, unable to think of anything else to say.

'A busy man, no doubt,' remarked Mrs Johnson briskly, and changed the subject abruptly. 'Your mother was very well when I telephoned her this morning, although she is still a little anxious about you—I thought that maybe you might like to telephone her this evening.'

'Thank you, Mrs Johnson.' Victoria was grateful for the kindly thought. 'Alexander rang her up twice and I did too, but it was a bit difficult not being able to speak loudly enough.' She got up and wandered over to the glass door leading on to the garden. 'May I go out and look round? It looks lovely; you and Uncle Gardener are both clever with flowers, aren't you?'

Her hostess joined her, and they stood on the minute lawn, rotating slowly, studying the flower beds which bordered it. Mrs Johnson said unexpectedly: 'He'll be back soon, child,' and patted Victoria's arm, and Victoria, who hadn't expected it and was taken unawares, asked like a child who needed to be reassured: 'Oh, do you really think so?'

'Depend upon it,' said Mrs Johnson. 'Come inside, I

want to show you my petit-point—I've almost finished it.'

The evening passed pleasantly and Victoria went early to bed in the small second-floor room at the back of the house. It was furnished with nice early Victoria bits and pieces and the curtains and bedspread were of sprigged chintz. Victoria, sitting up in bed, leafing through a copy of *Country Life* thoughtfully provided for her, sighed with pleasure. Really, the prospect of a few days in the charming little house with her two friends was very satisfying. 'I'm very lucky,' she told herself aloud, because it sounded more convincing like that and might serve to stifle the thought that it would be even nicer if Alexander were to come again soon. But she was beginning to learn that it was silly to speculate where he was concerned. She thumped her pillows rather peevishly. Probably at this very moment he was having a heavenly time with some gorgeous creature. After all, he might have rescued her in the most romantic fashion from her berserk patient, but anyone would have done the same. She reminded herself that he had called her his darling, and on this thought, went to sleep.

The days passed quietly. She accompanied her hostess shopping, mostly to Harrods, because Mrs Johnson had had an account there when she had first married and come to live in London, and had never seen a reason for discontinuing it. Victoria prowled around its fashion departments while Mrs Johnson, downstairs in the food section, pored over her weekly grocery list before joining her for coffee and then accompanying her to whichever department her fancy dictated. It was on their third visit to the store that Victoria discovered the bridal department and spent a delightful twenty minutes or so studying its display. 'Shall you wear white?' Mrs Johnson wanted to know, out of the blue.

Victoria put down a delicate coronet of orange blossom she had been examining; she could feel her cheeks grow hot under her companion's eyes, but she met them squarely enough. 'There's nothing like that,' she said carefully, 'really there isn't.' She looked almost pleadingly at her hostess. 'You see, nowadays it's—it's different...'

'I move with the times,' Mrs Johnson stated positively, 'but neither you nor this doctor of yours are what I would describe as permissive—have I the word right? I imagine it will be orange blossom and white satin once the pair of you can make up your minds.'

'No—yes, I don't know.' Victoria was conscious that she was putting up a poor show. She had always prided herself on being modern and sensible and just a little bit tough, and here she was behaving like a silly simpering creature in ringlets and a crinoline. 'Look,' she said, trying again, 'we haven't got as far as—as—well, we're friends, that's all.'

'Huh,' said her companion, 'that's not what your Uncle Gardener thinks.'

Victoria was appalled. 'He hasn't said anything,' she began. 'It's really no one's business,' she went on with some spirit.

'No, dear, I agree,' Mrs Johnson smiled at her kindly. 'And now I must go back to the food department. I quite forgot to order the ground almonds—Martha will never forgive me.' She said over her shoulder as she went: 'Shall we walk back home? It's such a lovely day.'

It was on Saturday morning, after breakfast, when Victoria chanced to look out of the sitting-room window to see the Mercedes draw up without sound before the door. The next instant she was on her way up to her room, her long slender legs making light work of the stairs. Once before her dressing-table mirror she began feverishly to put up her hair. 'How like him,' she muttered indistinctly through the pins she was holding between her teeth, 'to come at a moment's notice—and it would be on the very morning when I hadn't bothered to do my hair!'

She skewered the last of the fiery mass firmly to her head and began on the delicate task of applying lipstick. She hadn't quite finished when Martha's voice from the landing below besought her to go downstairs without loss of time. Even then, although her heart was pounding against her ribs in a most exciting fashion, she managed not to hurry—indeed, she paused long enough to spray her person with Dioressence before walking without haste out of her room and down the two flights of stairs to the sitting room. Alexander was standing at the garden end, viewing the flower beds with Mrs Johnson, but as Victoria went in he turned his head to look at her.

'And what possessed you to turn tail and run the moment you saw me?' he demanded flatly.

She halted by the door, her mouth a little agape because she hadn't expected that sort of greeting at all. Anyone else would at least have enquired about her bruises—it just showed how little interest he had in her, she told herself crossly, choosing to ignore the fact that he had made a considerable journey... Perhaps he hadn't, perhaps he had been in London...

She said snappishly, longing to be able to put her muddled thoughts into words and not having the time to do so: 'I didn't expect you.'

'No? But why bother to rush away and do your hair when you know that I like it hanging down your back?'

Her fine eyes flashed. 'I'm not in the habit of wearing my hair so just—just to please you!'

His face was bland. 'Neither are you,' he conceded silkily. 'As far as I remember it has usually been force of circumstances.' He smiled wickedly at her and Mrs Johnson said hastily: 'Well, you two will have plenty to tell each other, I've no doubt, and I must go to the kitchen and speak to Martha.'

'I'll go for you,' volunteered Victoria perversely even while she knew that to go out of the room, away from Alexander, even for a few minutes, would be agony. Mrs Johnson, luckily, took no notice of this silly remark, but went briskly to the door which the doctor was already holding open for her with a readiness not lost upon her. She gave him a bright glance as she passed him which he returned before shutting the door with quiet firmness behind her and turning to Victoria.

'Now, darling girl, why have you a bee in your bonnet? I thought you might be a little pleased to see me—and what do I find when I arrive? Without breakfast too—a crosspatch who turns and runs at first sight of me.'

Victoria's scowl changed all at once to motherly concern. 'No breakfast—oh, Alexander why didn't you say so! I thought—I didn't know if you'd come from Holland...'

He took a step or so nearer to her. 'Ah—the bee! I've been lurking in London all the week, ignoring you and that after saying I was going home. Worse, I have naturally been out every night with a succession of beautiful young women.' His smile held faint mockery as well as tenderness. 'Dear girl, I see that we have a long way to go yet.'

She didn't pretend not to understand, but it was the sort of awkward remark he was prone to make and which she was never sure how to answer. She gulped back what her over-ready tongue longed to say. 'I'll ask Martha to cook you some breakfast, you must be famished.' This sensible remark met with no answer and the decided twinkle in his eyes set her truant tongue off once more. 'Why did you come?'

'To see you, dear girl—to look at your bruises and find out how you are—and for this.'

Victoria felt herself whisked across the couple of feet which separated them and held fast in his arms. He was still smiling a little as he kissed her. It was a most satisfactory kiss, not at all like the featherlight salute he had given her in Sick Bay. It was, in fact, so satisfactory that he repeated it several times and each time she returned it happily. When at last they drew apart, she said, breathless:

'Alexander, oh, Alexander!' and then making a great effort to be sensible again: 'Your breakfast—I'll ask Martha.' She made for the door, but he put out a hand to hold her gently and turn her to face him again. 'Those bruises—they're all right? And your arms?' He examined them as he spoke, his face once more calm and impassive, so that he looked quite different from the man who had kissed her. He drew the scarf from her throat and examined that too and when he had finished, kissed her cheek, a light friendly kiss this time. 'Cured,' he pronounced. 'Fit enough to keep a dinner date.'

'Oh, but I can't—I still have to wear a scarf and if I go out—you know, where there are people, I have to have long sleeves.'

'That's easily solved. We'll go into the country and find somewhere small and remote, and if the landlord glowers at me for being a brutal husband who beats his wife, you'll have to smooth him down.'

She laughed because she was so happy she would have laughed at anything. 'You're absurd! Come along to the kitchen.'

Martha was already busy at the stove. 'You'll have had no breakfast, I'll be bound,' she stated cosily, 'and even if you did, it would have been very early.'

Alexander, invited to seat himself at the table, made an excellent meal, quite unabashed by the three women sitting round him and carrying on a lively argument with Mrs Johnson, who couldn't think why he didn't fly more often. It was all of an hour later when she asked him:

'Have you any plans? I suppose you're staying until tomorrow evening—have you a place to lay your head?'

He assured her that he had. 'And as for plans,' he continued, 'I rather thought I might take Victoria out into the country for the day, unless there is anything else she would rather do—or perhaps you have the day already booked?'

'Not a thing,' answered Mrs Johnson airily. 'You two go off together. Will you be back for dinner?'

'No, I shouldn't imagine so—some time before midnight…'

Victoria sat quietly. No one had asked her if she wished to go out for the day. Presumably it was taken for granted by everyone present that she would leap at the idea. She was scowling over this idea when Alexander turned to look at her, his eyes alight with laughter.

'Will you spend the day with me, please, Victoria? It has just occurred to me that you might not want to do so.'

She forgot to scowl. 'Why ever not?' she demanded, glowing under his look. 'I'll be ready in five minutes.'

It was ten, for she had reckoned without the one or two essential repairs she saw fit to make to her pretty, happy face. The dress she had on would have to do— she changed her shoes for a pair of new slingbacks she had just purchased, made sure her handbag contained all that was necessary for a young woman out for the day, and descended the stairs.

They were accorded a protracted send-off by the two elderly ladies to which the doctor listened with grave courtesy and Victoria, who was fond of them both, with loving tolerance. When at length the Mercedes slid away it was getting on for eleven o'clock.

'Lunch at Bibury?' enquired Alexander as he trickled the big car through the Saturday traffic.

Victoria summoned up her knowledge of the English countryside. She did it with some difficulty for her head was full of other, delightful thoughts. 'Bibury? Isn't that the Cotswolds? Aren't they miles away?'

'Yes and no. Only eighty-five miles or so, we shall get there in nice time for lunch—unless there is anywhere else?'

'It sounds lovely. I don't know the Cotswolds very well.'

'No? We'll go on to Malmesbury and Chippenham, come back along the A4 and find somewhere for dinner—Bray might do—there's a place by the river. I think it's called the Waterside.'

Having thus disposed of their day, the doctor applied himself to his driving, leaving Victoria to ponder the fact that he must either know his England very well, or was in the habit of making his plans very thoroughly before he started out. She ventured: 'Do you always know exactly where you're going, or do you work it out first?'

He cast her a sidelong glance. 'We have so little time together, dear girl, that I should dislike having to waste a minute of it poring over maps and trying to decide where we should eat.'

It was a satisfactory answer; she sat watching him drive, making, presumably, for the Bicester road. 'You know London very well too, don't you?'

'Yes. There would be no point in bringing the car over unless I made the fullest possible use of it.'

'Do you come over often?'

From the corner of her eye she saw his great shoulders heave with silent laughter. 'Is that a leading question, my darling girl? I come over to see you whenever I possibly can. Or didn't you know?'

Her heart bounced up into her throat; she swallowed it back and said sedately: 'That's very nice of you.'

This time his laughter exploded into a great roar. 'Victoria, you goose, there is nothing nice about it—I do it for purely selfish reasons. I like being with you, more...' he paused. 'Tell me,' he went on, 'for I never heard the whole story in one piece, how it was that you were so shockingly understaffed when that maniac attacked you.'

The telling of it took some time because he kept stopping her to ask questions. By the time she had finished they were well away from London and presently drove at a moderate pace through St Albans and then on to the A41 again, where the pace became not moderate at all. The Mercedes ate up the miles while they talked about Guernsey and hospital life and Mrs Johnson and then hospital again. It wasn't until afterwards that Victoria realised that he had asked her a great many questions which she had answered without much thought, even telling him how she felt about Jeremy Blake and how he had behaved towards her—quite civilly, in fact, as though he was sorry that he had been so unpleasant. Alexander grunted as she had said it, and it was afterwards too that she decided that the grunt hadn't been one of agreement but of disbelief. But at the time she hadn't noticed any of that, for her whole being had been given up to the pleasure of sitting beside him with the prospect of a whole day before them. 'This is fun,' she said impulsively, her face alight with happiness.

'Yes? I hoped you would find it so. When do you go back to work?'

It was a sobering thought. 'Two days' time—how quickly a week goes!' She looked at him as she spoke and went scarlet at his: 'That depends on who you are with.' He was, she thought, a trifle vexed, far too good at turning a harmless remark into something personal, she frowned as she thought it and he said to make her jump.

'Too personal, dear girl? Don't you know me well enough yet?' He was staring ahead as he spoke and didn't wait for her answer. 'All right, we'll have a harmless conversation about the countryside.' She thought his voice was a little too silky—perhaps he was annoyed, but after all, he had never actually said anything and he came and went—and for all she knew he might one day go for good... She followed his lead and they talked, happily enough, about the country they were passing through. They were going through Chipping Norton when she asked if they were getting near Bibury.

'Twenty miles or so—getting hungry?'

Victoria nodded and they drove in companionable silence until they drew up outside the Swan in Bibury. They ate their lunch without haste, discussing where they should go that afternoon and then, when they had finished, walked through the village to view the famous Arlington Row.

'Very picturesque,' pronounced Victoria, 'but I wonder what they're like in winter?'

'Snug,' said the doctor, and took her arm to walk her a little further along the road to see the ducks in the water before strolling back to look round the church, dim and cool and very peaceful, even in that peaceful little place.

They drove on presently, through Cirencester and on

to Malmesbury where they stopped to examine the Market Cross and take a closer look at the Abbey Church. The big car made light of the miles to Chippenham; they went straight through the town and on to Marlborough, where, because it was still too early for tea, the doctor declared his intention of going on to Savernake, where they found an hotel on the edge of the forest. 'A walk?' he suggested, and when Victoria agreed, got out of the car and went to help her out. It was a warm afternoon and they didn't hurry and when a patch of rough ground necessitated him taking her hand to help her, he didn't let it go again. His hand was cool and firm and reassuring. Victoria wished with all her heart that he might never let it go again. A silly wish, her common sense told her, but at that moment her common sense seemed powerless against the delightful, nonsensical thoughts flitting in and out of her head.

'You're not listening.' Alexander stopped and perforce she stopped too to say guiltily: 'I'm sorry—I was really, only I thought of something...'

His hand tightened on hers and he half smiled. She went on earnestly:

'Was it important? I really am sorry.'

'Don't be. Surely we are past the stage of apologising for being at ease with each other?'

Her mouth curved into a delighted smile. 'How lovely that sounds, as though...it's true too, I'm very at ease with you. I wonder why?'

He started to walk again. 'That's something I promise we'll discuss in a very short time. Let's walk as far as that oak ahead of us and then turn back. We can have tea at the hotel if you like.'

They had their tea, and Victoria, pausing in the middle of some engrossing topic, exclaimed: 'What a lot there is to talk about! I feel as though I shall never stop. Do you find it tiring—Father often says that we're more than enough to tire a saint.'

Alexander laughed. 'Don't worry, Vicky, you never tire me, nor will you ever do so,' and something in his look sent her heart singing once more.

They took to the by-roads on the way back and didn't reach Bray until after eight o'clock. The restaurant overlooked the river and was so delightful that Victoria regretted that she wasn't a little more dressed for the occasion, but when she went away to tidy her hair and take a good look at herself in the mirror, she decided that she didn't look too bad, despite her very simple dress, something of which her companion was already aware, for as she sat down he remarked, 'Collecting admiring glances again, Victoria? I can see that if I want you all to myself I shall have to find a dark cellar or drag you off to the remoter Highlands!'

'I like Scotland,' said Victoria, demurely. 'I wouldn't mind that at all.' She laughed at him across the table and he raised quizzical brows.

He said blandly: 'I'm tempted to take you at your word, my darling!' and gave her such a bright glance across the table that she went faintly pink under it, at which he smiled again and asked briefly: 'Now, what shall we eat? I believe the lobster cutlets are well spoken of—with a salad, perhaps?'

They ate their meal at leisure, talking about a great many things, and it was after ten o'clock when Victoria exclaimed: 'Should we be going, do you think? There's bound to be some traffic and it's almost thirty miles...'

Alexander agreed without demur, which rather annoyed her. Perhaps he had had enough of her company—breakfast, lunch, tea and dinner tête-à-tête might have been a little too much for him. She cast him an uncertain look and he said instantly: 'No, my reasons for taking you home are not those you have in mind—and don't ask me what I mean, because you know quite well. Where shall we go tomorrow?' He had shut the car door upon her and was settling his length beside her. 'I imagine it will be a fine day—shall we take a picnic? I have to get the Harwich ferry in the evening, I'm afraid, but I shan't need to leave London until eight o'clock.'

'Oh, you really want to spend the day with me again?' Victoria turned her head to look at him and the look on his face answered her question far more forcibly than his quiet 'Yes', she went on rapidly: 'What time shall I be ready? I'll bring the picnic.'

He was travelling fast through the last spring evening. 'Just before nine? How about exploring Essex?'

'Yes, let's. I'll be ready.'

'You go back on Monday, don't you?'

She had forgotten all about hospital. It seemed another world, far away and nothing to do with her. She said with a kind of surprise: 'So I do—I'd almost forgotten.' She subsided into silence, thinking that in no time at all, St Judd's would have swallowed her up again, just as though she had no life of her own. She sighed without knowing she had done so and he said sympathetically: 'Do you hate the idea? But you're not a girl to have a pointless life; you need to have something to do—am I not right?'

It was a little discouraging to find that he thought of her as a career girl when all she wanted was to be his wife and run his home and have several miniature Alexanders under her feet. She swept this beguiling daydream from her mind and said that yes, probably he was quite right.

He drew up before the house in Pimlico before midnight and although the light glowed through the transom over the front door, the rest of the house was in darkness.

He got out of the car with her and walked across the pavement and opened the door for her.

Before she could change her mind Victoria said: 'Would you like a cup of tea?'

He had lived long enough in England to accept the habit the English had of making pots of tea round the clock. 'Very much,' he answered, and followed her in.

They had their tea in the kitchen, drinking it from the blue-and-white-china mugs which hung on the scrubbed dresser, and Victoria felt happy because there was still so much to talk about and Alexander showed no signs of tiring of her company. She sat in Martha's comfortable, shabby armchair, watching the doctor washing the mugs and drying them and emptying the teapot before he returned them all to their proper places. He did it with unselfconscious ease as though he had done it many times before and thought nothing of it.

'Do you wash up at home?' asked Victoria.

He hung up the tea towel. 'Sometimes, if my housekeeper is away or I'm very late in and want something to eat after she's gone to bed.' He gave her a smiling glance. 'I'm quite domesticated.'

She saw that he was ready to leave; she got up off her chair and went with him to the door. 'It's been a lovely day, thank you, Alexander.'

He kissed her, far too briefly. 'Goodnight, Vicky, I'll be round in the morning.'

She watched him drive away, then went upstairs and got ready for bed, and still with her head full of him, went to sleep.

She was up early, but Martha was already in the kitchen. Victoria regaled her with the highlights of the previous day's outing and asked if she might have her breakfast early so that she could cut sandwiches.

'You'll have your breakfast at half past eight with Mrs

Johnson,' declared Martha firmly. 'Here's a cup of tea to keep body and soul together and leave me to get the picnic.'

Victoria accepted the tea. 'I can't let you do all that extra work,' she protested.

'Nonsense, I've nothing to do—now run along.'

Victoria got off the table. 'Well, thank you, Martha dear, but let me take up Mrs Johnson's tea for you and I can tell her about today.'

Mrs Johnson was awake, sitting up in bed, reading. She wished her guest good morning, took her tea and remarked: 'You'll be going out again today, I expect?'

'Well, yes, Alexander did ask me—do you mind? I feel very ill-mannered, but I couldn't tell you sooner because we didn't get back until nearly twelve.'

Her hostess smiled. 'My dear Victoria, I was so certain that your doctor would be here this weekend that I arranged to lunch with friends today.'

Victoria gaped at her. 'But supposing he hadn't turned up?'

'You would have accompanied me to Brigadier Groves' for luncheon, and a very dull time of it you would have had.' She shot a keen look at Victoria. 'I don't suppose you have a dull time with the doctor.'

'No,' said Victoria, a little breathlessly, 'I don't—there's such a lot to talk about.'

Mrs Johnson agreed gravely: 'Of course. He goes back this evening?'

'Yes.' Victoria went to the door. 'It's going to be a lovely day.' She found it impossible to keep the excitement out of her voice.

She went downstairs to hover restlessly about the little house and then into the garden. She had put on a sleeveless dress and discarded the scarf. The bruises were fading fast, but they still showed badly—still, if they were going to picnic there would be no one to see them, only Alexander. She examined her face in the sitting-room mirror, decided to take a cardigan to wear over her blue jersey dress and then went back into the kitchen to try Martha's patience, and presently, in Mrs Johnson's company, to eat a sketchy breakfast because she was afraid that Alexander might come early and she wouldn't be ready for him. He came at ten minutes to nine, putting an end to all her doubts, which she instantly avenged by declaring that she wasn't quite ready.

They spent the day, as he had promised, exploring Essex. Not the flat uninteresting part—the Mercedes carried them swiftly out of London and didn't slacken speed until Alexander turned off on to one of the lesser roads to Dunmow. They went through Great Bardfield and Finchingfield and so on to Saffron Walden, where they had coffee at the Rose and Crown after strolling along to see the old timbered and plastered houses. They turned east then, driving along the Suffolk border and exploring any lane which took their fancy. It was at the end of one of these lanes that they came upon high open ground, with a view of the rolling country around them, and even though it was early for lunch they decided to stop there. The sun was warm on the grass; they lay full length, side by side, hardly speaking until presently Alexander asked: 'Are you asleep?'

'No—just lazy. This is a heavenly spot.'

'Yes.' He rolled over on to his side to look at her and after a moment put out a hand and picked up her arm to examine the bruises.

'They're better,' she assured him. 'They look awful, but they don't hurt.'

He still held her lightly by the wrist. 'I cannot bear to see you hurt, Vicky dear. There's something I have to tell you. I shan't be able to come to England for a while, and I'm very bad at writing letters.'

He couldn't bear to see her hurt, her heart cried silently, and yet he could hurt her more than all the bruises. Was he trying to tell her that he wouldn't be seeing her again? The sun was warm on her, but inside she was suddenly cold. 'Me too,' she said lightly. 'They take up so much time, don't they, when there are other things to do.'

She lay waiting, hoping that he would tell her why he wasn't coming. All he said was: 'Will you miss me?'

'Yes.'

'Will you forget me?'

'No,' she spoke quietly staring up at the sky. 'I don't forget my friends even if I never see them again.' She sounded, despite the light tone, a little forlorn.

'You talk as though I'm going away for ever, you silly girl.' He spoke on a laugh and the temper which went with her hair stirred.

'I'm speaking generally,' she assured him coldly. 'It will be very pleasant to see you again if you should ever come to London.'

He didn't answer her but bent over and kissed her hard on the mouth. 'You're ridiculous,' he stated calmly, 'and you know it. You're being melodramatic and you know it.' He sat up. 'Let's have lunch.'

Victoria sat up too. Her voice, when she spoke, sounded cheerful, even in her own listening ears. 'Let's! I'm hungry and Martha's excelled herself.' They unpacked the picnic basket together and laughed and joked, and the little cloud of his departure hung between them so that although they talked as gaily as they had done earlier, it was, on Victoria's part at least, a little forced.

They drove on later and crossed the boundary into Suffolk and had a late tea at Long Melford, where they sat among the old rafters and beams of the Bull Inn, keeping up a steady flow of conversation, and if Victoria's was still a little too bright, the doctor's placid, friendly manner gave no indication of any unease on his part.

They were back in Pimlico before seven and to Victoria's surprise, when she asked him if he would like to come in he said: 'Of course, I must say goodbye to Mrs Johnson and Martha.'

His goodbyes were of necessity brief, though. Within five minutes he remarked with real regret that he would have to be on his way, and Mrs Johnson said: 'Of course—Victoria dear, see the doctor out.'

She stood at the street door with him, unable to believe that she wouldn't be seeing him—for how long?—perhaps he would forget her entirely. She put out her hand and said:

'Well, goodbye, Alexander. It was a gorgeous weekend, and thank you so much for the lovely times we've had. I—I expect we'll see each other some time.'

He stood looking down at her and she could see that behind his grave face he was laughing. 'What a very nice little speech,' he observed, 'like the end of a play.' He kissed her gently and without haste. 'Only do remember that it isn't a play, my darling; this is life—our life.'

A thousand and one answers crowded her throat, but by the time she had sorted them out he had got into his car and driven away. She went upstairs to her quiet little room and flung herself on her bed and cried her eyes out, not sure if she was very happy or acutely miserable.

CHAPTER SIX

GOING back to St Judd's wasn't as bad as she had expected it to be, probably because her head was so full of Alexander that she hardly noticed what was going on around her. The ward was full—too full—with beds down the middle and Sister Crow beside herself, what with the shortage of nurses; days off; Sir Keith's round imminent and some vital X-rays missing. She fell upon Victoria with a quite unusual welcome and spent ten minutes alternately grumbling and giving orders to put things right. Victoria, who knew exactly how she felt, and sympathised, soothed her as best she could and departed wardwards to get the nurses organised for the morning, which she did to such good effect that the round wasn't the catastrophe Sister Crow had prophesied. Indeed, Sir Keith was in high good humour and wasted quite a few minutes before the round began enquiring about Victoria's bruises and being so nice about it that she became a little pink under his kindly eye. Johnny she had already seen; he had clapped her on the back in a brotherly manner and told her that she didn't look too bad on the whole, and Jeremy Blake, when he arrived just before Sir Keith, was surprisingly pleasant and not too fulsomely friendly, as though he sensed that that was the last thing she wanted.

On the whole the morning went smoothly, and the afternoon, with the Old Crow off for a half day, went even smoother. By the time the part-time nurse came on at five, Victoria felt as though she hadn't been away at all, only, as she went off duty, she was conscious of feeling more tired than usual; too tired to go to the cinema with one of the housemen who met her on the way across the quadrangle. He was a nice young man—she quite liked him, but she was honest enough to admit to herself that if she went with him it would only be so that she might forget Alexander for an hour or two, and that was hardly fair on the boy. She thanked him with the friendly charm which had gained her so many friends in the hospital and went on her way to her room, where she stayed until supper time, writing a letter home. It took a very long time to write because she kept pausing to think about Alexander.

The days passed uneventfully; she spent her next days off with Mrs Johnson, who wanted to know how the doctor was, and Victoria was forced to explain as lightly as she could that she had no idea and didn't expect to, anyway.

'Easy come, easy go, these days, Mrs Johnson.' She summoned a laugh to make it sound genuine and was a little disconcerted when her hostess said: 'Rubbish. Oh, I'm sure you're right generally speaking, in this modern society—but that man's not modern society, nor will he ever be. Old-fashioned and full of tradition, I should imagine, with his own high standards to live up to.'

Victoria frowned. 'Yes, I'm sure you're right, but it isn't as though…I mean, we just enjoyed each other's company while he was in London.'

Mrs Johnson snorted with dignity. 'I am not a betting woman,' she informed Victoria, 'otherwise I would be prepared to make a wager… And how is the ward? Not too busy, I hope?'

Victoria had accepted the change of subject with relief, although she liked to talk about Alexander as a change from thinking about him all the time. He hadn't been mentioned again for the rest of her short visit.

It was towards the end of the second week that she noticed the change in Doctor Blake's manner towards her. He had remained cool, naturally enough, after their unfortunate fracas in the corridor, but now she noticed that he was trying to present himself in a better light. At first it was on the ward; instead of his usual hectoring manner, he had become positively mild and so polite on occasion that she had wondered what had come over him. Then, when they had encountered each other outside the ward, his manner was one of careful friendliness, although he remained a little aloof in his dealings with her, as though he sensed and understood her suspicion. But Victoria was by nature a kind-hearted girl and quick to forgive; she found herself unbending towards him, so gradually that she hardly noticed it herself and certainly failed to notice the small, secret smile of triumph he occasionally directed towards her. The other staff nurses had noticed the change too, and she had to put up with a certain amount of lighthearted teasing which she took in good part because she entertained no feelings towards him at all and found it all rather amusing. It wasn't until he asked her to go to the hospital Spring Dance with him that she realized that it wasn't amusing at all, for he seemed to take it for granted that she would accompany him, and when she refused— nicely—his face became quite ugly with ill-humour.

They had met by chance in one of the hospital corridors, going in opposite directions, and Victoria had been on the point of continuing her way when he asked with a sneer: 'You aren't hoping that Dutchman will turn up, are you? Out of sight, out of mind with him, Victoria, and if you'll take my advice...'

'No, I won't,' said Victoria sweetly. 'You're talking a lot of nonsense and I can't think why you should feel impelled to say all this to me. I haven't decided if I'm going to the dance yet, but I'm pretty sure I shan't. I'm sure if you look around you you'll find someone who'll be delighted to go with you.'

'No one as beautiful as you, Victoria.'

She frowned thunderously. 'Upon my word,' she began wrathfully, 'is that the reason you asked me? Of all the…' She turned on her heel. 'I'm going—I've a patient to fetch from OPD.'

She went on down the corridor, conscious that he was still standing where she had left him, staring after her. She would have to keep him at a distance, she thought angrily. It had been a mistake to accept his overtures of friendship, for he was so conceited that he had obviously imagined that she was more than ready to meet him halfway. She said loudly, 'The fool!' and met the shocked gaze of an old man sitting on one of the benches in OPD; he looked so put out that she felt compelled to stop and explain that it hadn't been he whom she had maligned.

It seemed that all her friends were going to the dance; moreover, they were all mystified as to her reasons for not going herself. She had given the excuse that she would be on duty that evening until eight o'clock, which was very rightly pooh-poohed by her friends, for the dance wouldn't get going until ten at the earliest, and when she put forward the suggestion that she had nothing fit to wear, her friend Judy from Children's got up from the bed in Victoria's room where they were, as usual, sitting, and wordlessly flung open the cupboard, allowing everyone there to see several dresses, all worthy of a hospital dance, hanging in it. And even to herself, Victoria refused to admit that the one and only reason why she wasn't going was because Alexander wouldn't be there with her, and no one else would do. She had done her best to forget him, or at least to think less of him, and it hadn't worked at all, in fact, the re-

verse. 'Absence makes the heart grow fonder' seemed
to have a considerable amount of truth in it, only it
seemed it didn't apply to everyone—everyone being Alexander.

She parried Sister Crow's questions easily enough;
that lady was going—it would be the last large hospital
function she would attend before her retirement and she
had no intention of missing it. She was full of the new
dress she had bought for the occasion, and beyond ex-
pressing faint surprise and relief that Victoria didn't
want an evening off on the day of the dance, she had
shown no curiosity as to why her staff nurse shouldn't
wish to go. As it was, Victoria saw the Old Crow off
duty at five o'clock on the great day and returned to the
evening's work, if not with pleasure, at least with a kind
of resigned highmindedness.

She had given out the medicines, sent the nurses to
supper, with the exception of Beauty, and was doing a
last-minute check to see that all her patients were as they
should be when she turned her head to see Alexander in
the ward doorway in deep, and judging from Beauty's
happy giggles, lighthearted conversation. She was at the
Major's bedside, and he, alert and keen-sighted enough
when it pleased him to be so, remarked: 'Ah, here's the
boy-friend, Staff—you'll be going to the dance after all.'
A remark uttered so smugly that Victoria vowed instantly that wild horses wouldn't drag her there. She was
still looking put out when the doctor came quietly down
the ward towards her. He wished the patients good evening as he passed them and enquired after the Major's
health before wishing her a good evening too, in a perfectly ordinary tone, just as though he had seen her several times that day already.

She had gone delightfully pink, but her 'Good eve-

ning, sir,' was as staid as the expression on her pretty face so that he smiled as he spoke.

'Poor Victoria, I'm always taking you by surprise, aren't I? But I did say I was coming back, or have you forgotten?'

They were standing in the middle of the ward, well out of range of the patients' ears. All the same, it was a little too public for her. She said austerely: 'No, of course I haven't forgotten,' and then, remembering where she was: 'I'm sorry, but I'm on duty—was there something you wanted?'

'You,' he said promptly, and the smile he gave her sent her heart soaring. 'I know you're on duty, but dress up as quickly as you can when you get off duty, we'll go and have a sandwich and then join the merry throng.'

Her heart was behaving in a most peculiar fashion. She willed it to calm down and opened her mouth to deny any desire to go dancing at such short notice, but he forestalled her with: 'Yes, I know, dear girl, I've no right to come at a moment's notice and spoil the nice quiet evening you intended to spend with a good book. I'll apologise here and now on my knees if you wish.' He paused and she saw with horror that he was prepared to do just that. 'Don't you dare!' she hissed. 'All right, I'll be at the front door at—at...' she did some swift calculating—'just before nine o'clock.'

He nodded. 'There's my darling girl. I'll go now, but tell me first why didn't you intend going—weren't you asked?'

'Of course I was asked!' She gave him an indignant stare.

'Then why didn't you choose to accept?'

She took refuge in a cool hoity-toity manner which set his eyes dancing wickedly. 'I'm so sorry, doctor, but

I must ask you to go now, I have quite a lot of work to do.'

'Shades of Sister Crow,' he murmured. 'You'll make a magnificent Ward Sister.'

He went back the way he had come, nodding easily to the patients and stopping once more, very briefly, to say a word to Beauty, still struggling with Mr Bray's intake and output chart. Whatever he said cheered her up mightily, for she came trotting up the ward in her squeaky shoes, anxious and eager to help Victoria. They were straightening the newest arrival's bed when she asked shyly: 'Are you going to the dance after all, Staff?' And when Victoria said a little absentmindedly—because she was deciding which slippers to wear—that yes, she was, Beauty went on to confide the marvellous news that she was going too.

'Who with?' asked Victoria, greatly intrigued.

'Jimmy from the Path Lab,' said Beauty, going a brilliant scarlet. 'We're friends.'

Victoria smiled at her kindly. 'Now, that's nice—he's a clever boy, is Jimmy, and so kind if we're late with specimens. I must remember to send you to the Path Lab more often, mustn't I?' and was rewarded by such a glowing face that her smile became even wider. 'I hope you have a fab evening,' she went on. 'Now run and do the rest of the water jugs as fast as you can—the others will be back at any minute now, and you can go when they are.'

She watched Beauty squeak happily down the ward and turned to meet Mrs Briggs, the part-time staff nurse, an understanding soul, who, as soon as Victoria told her that she was going to the dance after all, plunged into the business of the report without any of the usual casual talk accompanying it, so that Victoria was speeding off the ward not ten minutes later.

It was amazing what a lot could be done in half an hour or so if one really put one's mind to it. At the end of that period Victoria was kneeling before her dressing-table mirror in order to get a better view of her person while she looped her bright hair into a complicated style which, while taking an age to do, was well worth the effort. She had chosen her organza dress—a pale lime green with a pleated frill round its hem, long tight sleeves and a low-cut neckline. She stared into the mirror, making sure that there were no signs of the bruises she had received and was satisfied that there were none, then pushed her feet into gold slippers, sprayed herself liberally with Balenciaga's Quadrille, picked up her purse and her cloak and flew downstairs, because it was already nine o'clock. At least, she flew until almost the bottom of the stairs and then, not wishing to appear too eager, descended the last few steps in an unhurried manner so that by the time she reached the door she was almost in control of her breath again, although at the sight of Alexander, very elegant in his dinner jacket, her breathing defied her once more. Pink-cheeked, her eyes sparkling, she could find neither words nor breath with which to greet him.

If he was aware of her breathlessness he made no comment upon it but said easily: 'Good girl—I've got the car outside,' and whisked her out of the Home and into the Mercedes and was driving through the gates into the stream of evening traffic before she asked: 'Where are we going?'

'There's a place in Fleet Street. I thought we'd not better go too far.'

He had chosen well, for the restaurant wasn't too far from the hospital and although it was comfortably full he had had the forethought to book a table. They were served promptly and Victoria, whose appetite had failed her during the past weeks, did full justice to the beef in red wine and the trifle which followed it. They followed the claret they were drinking with coffee and then, without waste of time, drove back to St Judd's to join the dance. At first they didn't talk very much, content to dance together, and even when Victoria was claimed by Sir Keith and Alexander partnered first Matron then Sister Crow, these interruptions didn't seem to matter. It was while they were circling the ballroom in a sedate waltz—for the band had to cater for the older, more important guests as well as the younger, livelier ones—that Alexander asked:

'What are you doing tomorrow?'

'I have a day off.' Victoria tried to make her voice sound offhand and failed utterly, she was too happy. 'I'm going to Mrs Johnson's.'

'I'll be outside at nine o'clock and take you there. Do you suppose she would mind very much if I took you out in the afternoon?'

'No, I'm sure she wouldn't. She'll probably want you to stay to lunch!'

'I hope she does. Do you like museums, dear girl?'

Victoria hadn't quite expected that. She said carefully: 'Yes, but not Egyptian mummies or bones or things like that.'

'I promise there'll be no bones. Tell you what, we'll play safe and go to the National Gallery. I'm going back tomorrow evening.'

She had half expected that. She tilted her head back the better to look at him and found him staring down at her in a fashion which disconcerted her, it was so intense. Her voice was quiet. 'Yes, I thought you might be. You never stay long.'

His hand tightened a little. 'You miss me?'

Victoria lowered her gaze to his shirt front. 'Yes.'

He didn't answer and they danced in silence for a few minutes until he said softly above her head: 'I wonder why our Doctor Blake looks so murderous?'

She had forgotten all about him. 'He asked me to come to the dance with him.'

'Ah—and I take it you refused him in no uncertain terms.'

The band stopped and they strolled to one of the deep windows and stood looking out on to the uninviting and gloomy walls, lighted dimly by the bare windows of the wards. They stood side by side while she told him about Jeremy Blake and how she had thought he was sorry for his behaviour. 'But he's not, you know, not really...'

The man beside her gave a chuckle. 'I won't insult you by advising you to keep him at arm's length, Vicky. I daresay you'll be able to rub along—it won't be for long.'

'Oh? Is he leaving?'

'No, my darling, you are.'

Victoria opened her mouth to comment upon this surprising statement and thinking better of it, shut it again. The silence which followed seemed both deep and long so that she ventured: 'Am I? I didn't know.'

'Liar,' he remarked affably. 'What a pity we're in such a public place—we always seem to hold these interesting conversations at times when it is impossible to bring them to their logical conclusion.'

Victoria stared at the row of windows opposite them as though she had never seen them before and found them enchanting. She managed: 'What conclusions?

'Dear girl, I'm perfectly willing to kiss you here and now, in fact I can think of nothing I would rather do—the only reason I don't is because I feel that you might not find it a good idea.'

She found herself laughing. 'Alexander, you're hopeless, and I never know when you're serious...'

'Deadly serious, my darling.'

She flashed a quick look at his face and saw that he was. 'I think I'd like to dance again,' she said hastily.

She was only five minutes late the next morning and that was because she had met Home Sister on her way down and been asked to take a message to one of the maids in another part of the Home. 'Just my luck,' thought Victoria as she raced down the stairs and catapulted through the door, 'to meet Home Sister when there wasn't anyone else in sight to take her messages—why couldn't she have gone herself?'

Alexander was leaning against the car's shining bonnet with his hands in his pockets. He gave her a friendly smile as she approached him and said mildly: 'Hullo—what's upset you? If I didn't know you so well I might turn tail and run, you look furious.'

She smiled at once. 'I'm not really. I got held up for a few minutes, that's all, and I was afraid I'd be late and...'

'I'd not wait?' He opened the door for her. 'Dear darling girl, you're very unsure, aren't you? I shall have to remedy that.' He eased himself into the seat beside her. 'How nice you look. No one would think that you'd been dancing until the small hours.'

He didn't look as though he'd danced until the small hours himself, either, and he'd made a long journey before that too. 'Don't you get tired?' she asked.

He looked faintly surprised. 'Of course I do, after a heavy day, but I enjoy driving long distances and I like dancing with pretty girls too.' He gave her a faintly mocking glance. 'Or were you thinking that perhaps I can't stand such prolonged activities at my age?'

Victoria looked astonished. 'Your age? How absurd—
you're not old.' She turned in her seat and looked at him
carefully and her heart beat a good deal faster because
she loved him so very much, and over and above that,
he was remarkably good-looking. 'I'm not sure how old
you are,' she said at length. 'Thirty-two or three—you
can't be much younger because you're a consultant and
a lecturer—but you don't look any older...'

'I'm almost thirty-six, remember? Do you find that too
old, my darling?'

Victoria coloured brightly, when he gave her a sharp,
sideways look she didn't look away from his blue eyes.
'No, I don't.' She smiled deliciously at him and then, at
the gleam in his eyes, said: 'No, it's too public.'

He laughed then and switched on the engine and
guided the Mercedes gently through the hospital gates.
When he spoke again it was in a casual voice and about
the dance.

Of course he was invited to lunch; they found Mrs
Johnson in her little back garden, planting out stocks.
She hailed them with delight.

'I've two boxes of these and they have to go in today,
so you'll have to sit and watch me or go for a walk or
something. Lunch will be at one.'

'How about helping you?' suggested the doctor cheerfully, and Victoria, disappointed, found herself on her
knees, putting in stock plants with the meticulous care
Mrs Johnson insisted upon. They stopped for coffee after
an hour, sitting on the elegant wrought-iron furniture under the copper beech tree which took up the whole of
one corner, and Alexander, looking up from where he
was sprawled on the grass, remarked:

'You should always sit under copper beech trees,
Vicky, and wear a blue dress—you make a very pretty
picture.' And Victoria, to her annoyance, blushed for the

second time that morning and smiled a little shyly at him, thankful that their hostess was so absorbed in her coffee cup.

Lunch was a gay meal; there was the dance to discuss and the dresses to describe, and Mrs Johnson didn't once express surprise at Alexander's sudden appearance in London—indeed, she seemed to take it for granted. After the meal she urged them to go out at once while the traffic was slack. 'And tea's at four o'clock,' she added hospitably, 'but don't come back if you don't feel like it.'

The doctor thanked her gravely. 'In any case I shall see you again, I believe, for I shall bring Victoria back before I go.'

Mrs Johnson nodded briskly and ushered them out. 'Enjoy yourselves,' she advised them as Alexander started the car.

To Victoria's surprise, he drove straight to the Ritz Hotel. 'I thought we might walk from here,' her companion suggested. 'I can leave the car and we could come back here for tea.'

She nodded and as they got out of the car asked curiously: 'Do you always stay at this kind of hotel—big ones, I mean?'

'When I'm travelling, yes, but don't imagine that I can't make my own bed and cook a meal and sleep rough—but those things take time, and that's something I haven't much of, especially when I come over for a few hours.'

They crossed the road and walked, not too fast, towards Trafalgar Square and the National Gallery. It was a lovely day and as far as Victoria was concerned, there wasn't a cloud in her sky, nor would there ever be again. They talked—she had no idea about what, her sensible self pointed scorn at her blissful state; she ignored it and went up the steps of the National Gallery beside her companion in a lovely haze of feelings which, later on, would need sorting out, but which, at present, she was perfectly content to allow full freedom.

They wandered slowly from one room to the next, pausing when they saw something they liked; hurrying past everything else. They were studying a Gainsborough in a contemplative silence, lulled by the complete emptiness of the room they were in and its almost cathedral-like atmosphere. 'It's nice,' Victoria decided, her head on one side. 'Do you suppose they had been married long when it was painted?'

'Probably not—why do you ask?'

'Well, I know they're not looking at each other, but you can see that they're—serene; sure of themselves— quite happy.'

She glanced at him as she spoke and found herself unable to take her eyes from his. After a long moment he took her by the arm and turned her round, away from the portrait, to face him.

'I doubt if I shall ever be sure of myself as far as you're concerned,' he remarked quietly, 'and serenity is the last feeling I have when I'm with you. Rather, you stir me up...but of this I am sure, I am completely happy.'

Victoria drew a breath. 'So am I.' She spoke simply; the words had tumbled out without her even thinking about them, but it didn't matter.

He pulled her close. 'Oh, my dear delight,' he said softly, and kissed her and kissed her again because they were still alone and there was, just for a brief space, all the time in the world.

Presently he loosed her just a little. 'I want you to come to Holland, Vicky, and meet my parents. I should like to take you back tonight, but that's impossible isn't

it? But will you go to Matron and resign this evening?
Tomorrow morning I suppose it will be. When you leave
I'll come and fetch you and take you home—your future
home in Holland.'

'But,' said Victoria, 'that won't do. I shan't have a
job...'

'You won't need one, darling, you'll be my wife.'

She blinked at him, smiling a little. 'But you haven't
asked me,' she reminded him. There was still no one
else there but themselves in the vast room so that Alexander was able to take his time about it in a manner
which satisfied Victoria completely. Presently he said:

'I'll write to your father—you'll want to marry from
your home, won't you? We can arrange that later.' He
kissed her swiftly and let her go as a steady tramp of
feet heralded the approach of sightseers—they had time
to turn round again and study the Gainsborough before
a large party of school-children poured into the room.
Victoria, giving a startled look at them over her shoulder, responded to Alexander's touch on her shoulder and
was led rapidly away to another even larger room, round
which they strolled, happily unaware of the treasures
around them, while they discussed, as sensibly as possible, how they should order their immediate future.

'I'm rather booked up with work for the next few
weeks,' explained Alexander. 'I'll be able to manage an
odd day here and there, but no more than that. We'll
have to wait for a month before we can be together,
Vicky, and even then although we shall see each other
every day, I shall be tied by the practice. But you will
be staying with my mother and father and you will get
to know them, and as soon as we can arrange things we
will go over to Guernsey for the wedding. Will you like
that, dearest?'

Victoria liked it very much, although she didn't care

where they married. She supposed that her mother would prefer her to have a big wedding. She frowned a little, trying to imagine herself going down the aisle of the Town Church in St Peter Port, completely dwarfed by her three tall and striking sisters. A very quiet wedding might be much nicer.

'You're frowning,' said Alexander. 'Why?'

She shook her head and smiled instantly. 'Nothing. It won't be quite a month, you know. I can get two days off in the last week and there'll be a few days' holiday due to me. It'll be nearer three weeks.'

There was no one about. He kissed her once more. 'Three weeks too long. Let's walk in the park.'

They spent the remainder of the afternoon strolling up one path and down the next. There seemed such a lot to say and only a very limited time in which to say it. They were both surprised when Alexander looked at his watch and discovered that it was getting on for five o'clock, so that they quickened their steps and went back to the hotel and had a rather hurried tea under the eyes of a waiter who served them with an understanding smile which neither of them noticed.

Back outside the house in Pimlico Victoria asked: 'Shall I tell them?' She was getting out of the car and Alexander caught her hand and held it. 'Or do you want to keep it a secret?' she added, rather breathless under his look.

'Why should I want to keep it a secret? I'm in the mood to stand in the middle of the road and proclaim my happy state to anyone who would listen.'

'Don't you dare do any such thing,' said Victoria severely. 'Come inside.'

Mrs Johnson, when they told her, was delighted but not surprised, nor for that matter was Martha, who embraced them both with happy abandon and said wisely:

'Well, anyone could see with an eye in their head which way the cat was jumping. Made for each other, you are.' She beamed at them and then at a signal from Mrs Johnson went to fetch the glasses while Mrs Johnson retired to some secret place of her own, to return with a bottle of champagne. 'Just a drop,' she urged Alexander. 'I'm sure it won't affect your driving,' and handed him the bottle to deal with. They drank their toast in the sitting room and then the two older ladies retired to the kitchen on what they described as pressing business, leaving Victoria and Alexander together.

'They're dears, aren't they?' asked Victoria. She was standing at the open window, looking out on to the garden, feeling very happy and at the same time very sad because in a very few minutes Alexander would have to go and she didn't know how she was going to be able to bear not seeing him. 'When will you come?' she wanted to know forlornly, and was swung round and held so tightly that her ribs ached.

'I'm not sure—you see, as well as the practice I have beds in two hospitals and several in nursing homes. Besides, I've two short trips—to Germany and France— but they're only for a day or two. All the same I'm not going to give you any dates, my darling, in case I get held up, but I promise you I'll come as soon as I can.'

She nodded into his shirt front, being a reasonable girl and knowing moreover that members of the medical profession couldn't always call their time their own. 'Flying visits?' she murmured wistfully.

'Flying visits. I'm going now, Vicky.' He kissed her hard and then gently and with a tenderness to make her heart turn over. Before she could as much as say goodbye, he had gone. She heard the car start up, but she didn't go to the window overlooking the street because she knew that he didn't want her to.

She went back to the hospital herself an hour or two later, having eaten supper with Mrs Johnson and resisted a strong temptation to telephone her mother and tell her all about it, but Alexander had said that he would write and it seemed to her right to wait until he had done so. He was, she guessed, a man who was a little old-fashioned in many ways and conventional as well, especially over important things, like getting married. She smiled as she thought it, for in a great many ways he wasn't conventional at all; being married to him was going to be quite wonderful. She dreamed her way back to St Judd's in the taxi which her kind hostess had insisted on calling for her, and into the Home and her room, on the way to which she met several of her friends who looked at her happy face and exchanged speaking glances with each other. They came and drank their bed-time tea in her room later, but managed, with commendable self-control, not to ask her any questions.

The ward was busy the next morning when she went on duty, moreover it was Sir Keith's round, and several of the newer patients, not long enough on the ward to know about Sister Crow's wishes on this all-important event, untidied their beds after they had been made immaculate and one of them had even smoked a forbidden cigarette under the bedclothes, half suffocating himself in the consequence, which necessitated a great deal of last-minute activity on the part of the already harassed nurses. Poor Mr Bates was feeling sick again, too. Victoria, ironing out the wrinkles in the morning's work, had little time to think about herself or Alexander, although every now and then a glow of pure happiness swept over her. Despite the morning's rush she had managed to get down to Matron's office earlier and when she offered her resignation, Matron had smiled quite nicely and said:

'Well, Staff Nurse, we shall be losing a good member of our staff, but I daresay you will make Doctor van Schuylen an excellent wife.'

Which had surprised Victoria very much, for she hadn't realised that anyone had noticed. She looked enquiringly at Matron, who went on: 'Doctor van Schuylen telephoned me just before you asked for an appointment to see me, Staff Nurse.' She nodded dismissal. 'I'll get the office to let you know when your leaving date falls due. Give them the details as you go out, will you?'

Victoria had done so gleefully, thinking as she did it that when she had time she would sit down and think out a few details for herself too. Should she go home first, for instance, or should she get one of her friends to store most of her luggage until she could fetch it? It all rather depended on what Alexander and she could arrange between them, and that would have to wait, probably until she was in Holland. She went through the hospital, back to the ward, her head full of delightful, half-formed plans, to be instantly discarded as she was met by the Old Crow, as usual in a state of pre-round nerves and full of commands and contradictions. Victoria hurried up and down the ward, urging the nurses to do their best; cajoling patients to keep tidy, get back into bed, refrain from starting on their bowls of fruit until after the round, and refrain too from the loud cheerful exchange of news and views they were wont to pass up and down the ward. When finally she had the situation more or less to Sister Crow's liking there were the mislaid forms and notes to find—these had a most extraordinary habit of disappearing on round days. Johnny and Jeremy Blake both had a bad habit of taking them off the ward for some reason or other and a certain number slipped down behind beds, got pushed behind anything handy in Sister's office, or, very rarely, were actually screwed up and flung into the waste-paper basket. It was most peculiar, thought Victoria, running a practised, exploratory hand behind the filing cabinet in the office, how doctors could write reams of notes and then carelessly lose them. She retrieved the last missing sheet, added it tidily to the pile of notes standing ready for Sir Keith's perusal should he so wish, and retired to the linen cupboard to tidy her hair and powder her nose, to appear, very neat as to person, on the ward a few minutes before the familiar routine between the consultant and the Old Crow was due to begin.

The round passed off without incident and the rest of the day went smoothly, as did the ensuing days. Victoria, buoyed up by the short but entirely satisfactory notes which Alexander dashed off in his untidy handwriting, answered them at length; made plans, which, as they were largely surmise, were both impractical and highly imaginative, and had long talks with her family over the telephone almost every evening. They had taken the news of her impending marriage with excitement but a complete lack of surprise; her mother made sensible suggestions about luggage and her passport and the right clothes to take and her father contented himself with saying that as long as she was happy, he was happy too and that Alexander had struck him as being a very sound fellow. Her three sisters, who had taken it for granted that she was going to have an enormous wedding in the Town Church and brushed aside any suggestions to the contrary, clamoured to know what they were to wear.

It was after a particularly lively session on the subject of bridesmaids that Victoria recollected that she and Alexander weren't even officially engaged. This thought brought another in its train. Supposing his parents didn't like her—even hated her, and tried to persuade him that she wasn't suitable? That he wouldn't be persuaded she

was sure, but they could show their disapproval in a
dozen different ways. She brooded about it for the rest
of the evening and was still full of unexpected doubts
when she went to bed, and finally to sleep.

The doubts were dispelled the following morning by
a letter from Alexander's mother, who wrote charmingly
to invite her to stay with them in Leiden. The letter,
although vague as to dates and lacking all mention of
marriage between her and Alexander, was sincere and
friendly. Victoria heaved a sigh of relief and wrote a
careful reply before she went back on duty. There had
been no letter from Alexander for two days now, but
probably he was away, and there was always the evening
post to look forward to. She went to the office and took
the report and watched Sister Crow go off duty for the
half day, then went to start the medicine round.

She had done the final evening round, written the report and was filling in the last of the charts when Jeremy
Blake came into the office and asked her with cool ci-
vility if he might write up a new patient's notes.

'Of course,' said Victoria readily. 'Is it Mr Hill? His
chart's here.' She handed it over as she spoke and went
on with her own work in a silence broken presently by
the telephone. It was the head porter, a nice old man on
the point of retirement. He wheezed chestily into her ear.
'Staff? When you come off duty you're to come down
to the front hall—there's someone here...'

Alexander's voice, very calm, almost careless, took
over.

'Dear girl, come straight here. Are you busy?'

'No, not really, just waiting for the night nurses.' She
tried to make her voice as calm as his and failed utterly.

'Alone?'

'No.' She heard his chuckle.

'Shall I give three guesses?'

'No. I'll come down as soon as I can.'

She replaced the receiver, very conscious of Doctor Blake's sharp eyes, and returned to her charts.

'Ah, the boy-friend,' he observed smoothly. 'He's been gone a long time, hasn't he? A week—ten days? A busy man, it seems.' Victoria took no notice. 'Perhaps not as busy as he makes out,' went on Doctor Blake nastily. 'It's none of my business, but these foreigners, however charming, aren't always to be trusted.'

Victoria's fine eyes flashed and sparkled with temper, but her voice was commendably cool. 'As you say, it's none of your business, and I should look out if I were you or you'll find yourself being sued for libel,' she paused, 'or is it defamation of character? Anyway, it's something quite severe which wouldn't do you or your career any good, and,' she added severely, 'I should hardly describe you as someone to be trusted.' She nodded her beautiful head at him with a severity which matched her tone, finished the last chart and turned to greet the night nurses.

The desire to spend a few minutes on her face and hair before going downstairs to Alexander was strong, but not nearly as strong as her wish to see him as soon as she possibly could. She raced down the corridor and the stairs, and arrived, a little breathless, in the front hall. Only Alexander was there, and the head porter in his little box had his back to them. She flew into Alexander's arms to be kissed in such a manner as to make nonsense of tidy hair and fresh lipstick.

'How long?' she asked.

'My dear girl, here I am, just this minute arrived and you're asking with every sign of eagerness when I'm going again!'

She chuckled. 'Don't be tiresome. You know exactly what I mean.'

He kissed her again by way of answer. 'Tomorrow evening,' he told her. 'Go and put on something and we'll go and eat.'

They went to the restaurant in Fleet Street again, and ate steak and kidney pie and chocolate mousse, then sat over their coffee for a very long time while Victoria told him about his mother's letter and then, rather shyly, about her sisters' excitement about the wedding.

He listened to her with a half smile on his face and when she had finished, said: 'They'll have to wait a week or two until we can arrange the date. When you're in Holland, dear love, we'll go through my commitments together and fix on a day. I shall be able to manage a couple of weeks' holiday, I think. I've told my secretary to cram as much into the next week or so as she can.'

Victoria poured them both more coffee. 'I had my leaving date from the office this morning.' She mentioned a day just over two weeks distant. 'I don't think I'll go home first, one of the girls has said she'll take my heavy luggage and keep it for me. Will that be all right? I mean if I come over to Holland right away?'

'I'll fetch you—you leave on a Friday, don't you? I can't get over until the Saturday, so could you spend another night in hospital or go to Mrs Johnson, do you suppose?'

'I'll go to Mrs Johnson. But wouldn't it save you a lot of trouble if I went over to Holland and you met me there? I can quite well…'

'I'm sure you can, Vicky, but I've no intention of letting you do so. I'll fetch you as I said, on the Saturday.' He put down his cup. 'And now we'll drive round for a little while, shall we? Unless you're tired and want to go back to the Home?'

Victoria picked up her handbag. 'Sometimes,' she remarked austerely, 'you make very silly remarks.' She accompanied this censure with a look which left no doubt as to her willingness to be driven round for as long as he might wish.

He smiled. 'Don't tempt me,' he said softly. 'I shall put you down outside the Nurses Home door at midnight and not a moment later.'

He was as good as his word; she went sleepily to bed, in a happy dream that for her, at the moment, had no ending.

She had a split duty the next day and tore off duty to scramble into a jersey dress and do her hair and face. It was beautiful weather, although she had scarcely had time to notice it during the morning, but now, getting into the car beside Alexander, she let out a great sigh of content as he said: 'We'll run out into the country—I think we can just manage it. There's a place called Cole Green, only about twenty miles, we might get a late lunch there.' He glanced at his watch. 'We'll have to come straight back, but it's better than London on a day like this.' He smiled down at her, a warm, tender smile which lighted up his whole face. 'Have you been busy, my love?'

She recounted the morning's work briefly and then demanded to know about his own work in Holland. The subject kept them occupied until they reached Cole Green where the inn offered them a good lunch. It was as they were coming to an end of it that Alexander told her that he wouldn't be able to get over to see her again: 'Not if I'm to get a week or two later on, my darling—besides, I want some leisure when you are in Holland. I'll telephone you whenever I can and write often.'

Victoria thought of the brief scribbles he had sent her from time to time and smiled gently. 'That'll be nice—your letters are so newsy,' and when he laughed, added: 'I write you pages and pages.'

'I only write for one reason,' he assured her, 'to tell you that I love you—the news can wait.'

'In that case,' said Victoria, a little nettled, 'I shall send you a postcard now and then.'

'Don't dare—I love your letters, I've kept them all and always shall. And now we must go, dear love.'

It was dreadfully dull without him again, especially now that she knew she wouldn't be seeing him until she left St Judd's. Even his frequent telephone calls and scant letters did little to speed the days passing so slowly. The ward wasn't busy either, so that she had time on her hands to think of him constantly. But suddenly there were only a couple of days left and she could at last pack her cases, do some last-minute shopping, say goodbye to her friends and telephone her family for the last time before she left England. Sister Crow bade her goodbye with a good deal of tut-tutting as to the future. Johnny hugged her and wished her luck in a way to warm her heart, as did the Major and Mr Bates. The nurses had clubbed together and given her a delicate china dish which she promised to use every day. Only Jeremy Blake said nothing. She was actually on the point of going off duty for the last time when he waylaid her in the corridor once more.

'Well, well,' he began in what she was forced to admit was a friendly manner, 'so you're leaving us for a rosy future, presumably. Let's hope it is.'

Victoria had paused, because he had looked friendly; now she started to walk on, away from him. 'I've no doubt of it,' she said without rancour because, after all, nothing he said could annoy her any more; she would never see him again after that evening. She smiled to herself, remembering how Matron had told her that should she ever wish to return, there would always be a place for her. She could imagine Alexander's views if she suggested working after they were married! All the same, it was nice to know that she hadn't burnt quite all her boats. The thought pulled her up short, for it smacked of disloyalty to Alexander. She dismissed the subject from her mind and turned to the contemplation of her happy future.

CHAPTER SEVEN

THE boat was crowded. Whichever way they turned, they were hemmed in by people, so that any conversation they had was of a purely impersonal nature. They had had dinner on the way down from London—and a good thing too, said the doctor, surveying the packed tables in the ship's restaurant.

'We're going to your cabin, Vicky,' he decided, 'I'll get someone to bring us some coffee there and then leave you to have a good sleep. We dock quite early—half past six, but we'll breakfast on board so that it will be quieter by the time we leave.'

Victoria agreed, not caring in the least what they did, so long as they did it together. She followed him down to her cabin, drank the coffee he poured for her, and after he had bidden her a most satisfactory goodnight and instructed her to apply to him in his cabin next door if she needed anything, she was left to sleep. She had hardly closed her eyes the night before for excitement and the moment she laid her head on the pillow she slept, not to wake until she was called the following morning. Alexander was knocking on her door long before she was ready. She called an indistinct 'come in' through a mouthful of hairpins, which he instantly removed the better to wish her good morning and then sat down on the berth while she rapidly started to put up her hair, ramming the pins in at a great rate.

The sun was up, shining over the complex of Euraport as they got into the car. Victoria, who had expected black and white cows in green fields and distant pastoral views, tried not to show her disappointment at the scene around them, which could have been Tilbury Docks or Merseyside. They were already clear of the Hoek, going towards den Haag along the main road, when Alexander said: 'Don't take any notice of the view, darling, it will get better very soon, once we are away from this industrial area.'

As indeed it did; presently she was exclaiming over the shape of the farm buildings, the extreme smallness of some of the houses in the villages they passed through, and the flatness of the surrounding countryside.

'They're quite right, you know,' she observed to her companion. 'It's just like a soup plate—is that the Hague in front of us? What a long way one can see, it makes everything seem very close by.'

'Den Haag,' he corrected her. 'Yes, it's not far, you see, it's such a small country.' He gave her a quick sidelong glance. 'Do you suppose you could be happy in it, darling?'

Victoria had no doubts; she smiled at him enchantingly. 'I don't mind where I live as long as you're there,' she told him, 'and I'm sure I shall like Holland. I can't wait to see where you live.'

'Well, dear girl, you'll have to—I'm taking you straight to my consulting rooms to pick up any letters or messages my secretary may have left for me and then driving you on to my father's house in Leiden. Tomorrow I'll take you to Wassenaar and you shall look over your future home and tell me what you think of it.'

She stifled disappointment; she very much wanted to see his home in Wassenaar, but his consulting rooms would be the next best thing, and he was, after all, free for the rest of the day. She longed to be with him all the time; his parents were strangers. Supposing they found that they didn't like her? Supposing she didn't like them? She sighed without knowing she did so and he rather surprisingly answered her thoughts.

'Don't panic, my darling, Mother and Father are looking forward to your stay; I've told them a great deal about you and I shall be coming over to see you each day and every weekend.'

They were in the suburbs of den Haag by now, travelling fairly slowly, presently they came to the heart of the city and Victoria craned her neck, anxious to miss none of the sights Alexander was pointing out to her.

'This is called Lange Vijverburg,' he explained. 'My rooms are in one of the streets leading from it.' He turned the car as he spoke and drove down a narrow thoroughfare lined with tall houses, before one of which he stopped. Victoria went up the steps leading to the heavy wooden door without speaking and waited while he unlocked it. Inside the hall was lofty and narrow with an elaborately plastered ceiling and plain walls. The floor was tiled and a staircase at the further end led to the floor above. Alexander opened a door close to where they were standing and stood aside for her to go in. A waiting room, an opulent one, she was quick to see, with a businesslike desk in one corner and several comfortable chairs scattered around. The doctor gave it scant attention, however, but took her arm and led her across the thick carpet to a door in the opposite wall and ushered her in. His consulting room was comfortable and very tidy, with shelves of books and an outsize desk. It was perhaps a little sombre, but nonetheless it exuded an atmosphere of calm and security which she knew from experience most patients both expected and needed. She toured the room slowly, picking things up and putting them down again and peering at the books, presently she went to the window and looked out. The street outside was quiet because it was Sunday, but she fancied that even on a weekday it would preserve its bygone air of unhurried peace. She turned round and found Alexander close behind her.

'I like it. I've often wondered where you worked. Now I know, and when I think of you the right background will be there.' She gave him a bewitching smile as she spoke and was at once crushed tightly to him, to be kissed and kissed again.

'Dear love,' said the doctor, 'very soon you won't need to think of me, because we shall be together against any background you may choose.'

Victoria laughed at that and lifted her face to kiss him. 'What would you like me to do?' she asked, trying to be sensible. 'Do you not have letters to read and suchlike things to do?'

He released her, smiling. 'Yes—will you sit here while I go through them? I don't suppose there's much to worry about.'

She sat as still as a mouse, watching him as he sat at his desk and went quickly through the pile of letters upon it. Some he put on one side; some he threw straight into the waste paper basket, and some he frowned over and switched on his dictaphone and spoke into it. In Dutch, of course—Victoria, who hadn't heard him speak that language before, sat fascinated, listening to him. It sounded nonsense; she doubted if she would ever be able to speak a word, let alone the whole language.

When he had finished he said in English: 'I leave instructions for my secretary if there's something that needs attending to—then she can get on with it as soon as she comes in in the morning, it saves us both a great deal of time and saves the poor girl reminding me to do something I might forget.'

Victoria nodded and then, 'You seem different when you speak Dutch.'

'Well, I'm not, my love. As soon as you've learned a little of the language you won't think that. We'll speak English together as much as possible if you would prefer that, but I should like you to learn my language, it will be so much easier for you—and think how hard it will be on our children if we don't share the same tongue.'

She went a very beautiful pink. 'Oh—I hadn't thought of that. Won't they be clever, speaking two languages at once?'

The doctor put down the paper in his hand and came over to her. 'The prospect fills me with pleasure,' he declared, and kissed her several times before he went back to finish what he was reading.

He was done in another ten minutes or so and they got back into the car and drove on through the city, stopping at a small café to drink coffee as they went. Once on the motorway, Victoria could see Leiden against the near horizon; it seemed no time at all before they were threading their way through the corkscrew streets. 'Breestraat,' Alexander informed her, 'and now we're crossing the Rapenburg Canal—the university is just behind those houses.'

'Yours?' Victoria wanted to know.

He nodded. 'And now we're going west towards the sea. My father's house is just outside the city. I've taken you the long way round so that you could have a quick glimpse.'

He turned off the main street and went smoothly along a tree-lined road. The town houses seemed to have been left behind, although here and there there were villas. Victoria found them rather elaborate and not very old, but the house at whose gate they turned in was another matter—not large, but square and solid with no-nonsense windows and a beautifully carved front door. It had a garden to match it too, very neat and formal, the beds filled with orderly rows of flowers and the whole circumvented by a high iron fence partly screened by shrubs. They came to a halt before the door and were getting out when it was opened. The man who stood waiting for them seemed very old to be Alexander's father; his hair was snow white and his shoulders were bowed. She was halfway up the shallow steps when the doctor said in a low voice: 'This is Jaap, he's been with us—er—man and boy. That's the right expression, is it not?'

He clapped the old man gently on the shoulders and spoke to him in his own language, then said to Victoria: 'He doesn't speak any English, but he knows all about you.'

Victoria extended a hand, to have it wrung with surprising strength by Jaap, who beamed at her, gave her an unintelligible welcome and led the way indoors. The hall was narrow and lofty, just as the hall at the consulting rooms had been, only unlike it, this was handsomely panelled in dark oak below an ornately plastered ceiling. Doors led from it on both sides and the second one on the right was opened by Jaap, to disclose a square, sunny room overlooking the back of the house, furnished in the Beidermeier manner, the rather heavy furniture offset by the muted browns and creams of the curtains and covers. The floor was of highly polished wood, covered for the greater part by a carpet patterned in a rich terra-cotta and olive green, which colours were picked out by the china in the display cabinet along one wall and the various table lamps scattered around. A comfortable sofa took up the space before the large hearth, flanked by a number of comfortable easy chairs. From two of these rose Alexander's parents.

Victoria had often tried to imagine them, for she hadn't liked to question him about them too much, and although his father was very much as she had expected, being in fact an older edition of his son, his mother bore no resemblance to her imaginings, for she was shorter than Victoria herself with what could only be described as a cosily plump figure. Her hair, which had been very fair, was now heavily silvered and beautifully dressed, as was her person. She smiled as she stood up and her rather severe good looks were immediately transformed by its warmth. Alexander crossed the room to her, kissed her soundly, wrung his father's hand and turned to Victoria with a smile of such pride and tenderness that any lingering doubts she might have had were instantly melted.

'Mother, Father, this is Victoria.' He caught her by the arm and gave it a reassuring squeeze. 'Victoria, my mother and father.'

She was welcomed with a kindness she hadn't quite expected. Before she knew where she was, she was sitting beside her hostess on the sofa telling her about the journey. Alexander interrupted them presently to offer them sherry and the conversation became general until Mevrouw van Schuylen invited her to go upstairs to her room. 'Alexander will fetch your luggage and Jaap can take it up for you,' she stated comfortably as she led Victoria up the straight, steep staircase.

The landing above was as narrow as the hall with a similar number of doors leading from it, and at its end was a small archway through which she could see more doors and a little flight of stairs. Mevrouw van Schuylen saw her interested look and explained: 'There's a wing behind the house—you can't see it from the front, and another floor above us. The house is really too big for us now, but we have a large family'—she paused to smile. 'Alexander will have told you—two daughters and two sons as well as he—and of course, grandchildren. Besides, the house will become Alexander's one day; it has belonged to my husband's family for a very long time and both he and Alexander love it dearly.'

She opened a door as she spoke and invited Victoria to enter. The room was of a fair size, facing the front garden, with a tranquil view of the fields beyond the road from its windows. It was furnished prettily with Regency furniture with a couple of small easy chairs and a davenport against one wall. Victoria saw that it held notepaper and a small silver ink standish, ready for her use. The bedspread was of pale blue, as were the chair covers and the curtains, and Victoria was charmed when her hostess told her that she had been given the room because its colour scheme would become her. 'Such pretty hair,' went on Mevrouw van Schuylen, 'and you are even lovelier than Alexander told us. I'll leave you for a few minutes,' she added kindly. 'Come down when you are ready, Victoria. There is a bathroom next to this room—regard it as your own, and if there is anything you should want, you will please ask.'

She went away with a backward smile over her shoulder, and Victoria, after a hasty inspection in the mirror, wasted a few minutes gazing out of the window, looking at several delightful flower paintings on the walls, and inspecting the bathroom, a luxurious apartment which, despite the age of the house, lacked for nothing in modern amenities. Some ten minutes later she went downstairs again, feeling a little shy; it had been easy enough to enter the sitting room with Alexander beside her, but on her own she felt a vague reluctance—entirely wasted, as it turned out, because Alexander was waiting for her in the hall, standing casually with his hands in his pockets, staring at a family portrait, dark with age. He went to meet her as she reached the bottom of the stairs.

'Come and see the garden before lunch,' he invited

her in a matter-of-fact voice which made nonsense of her shyness, and tucked her hand under his arm and led her through another door at the end of the hall which in turn led into a conservatory of some size, opening on to the garden.

It was bigger than she had supposed and there was a small gate in one corner leading to a sunken garden with a pool in its centre and a number of small ornamental trees around its borders. It was completely hidden from the house; a small sunny refuge, and very peaceful.

'Oh, this is lovely!' exclaimed Victoria. 'Whoever designed it? Someone who liked peace and quiet, I should suppose—why, you could hide here all day and no one would know.'

'I don't know if the man who built it shared that opinion,' said Alexander. 'Probably he had it made so that he could escape from his wife and children when they got too much for him. I daresay he was a man of leisure, unable to escape to work from the family circle.'

'Well,' burst out Victoria indignantly, 'what a thing to say—if you imagine you'll be able to duck domestic responsibilities...' She got no further, for he engulfed her in an embrace and kissed her breathless so that she was unable to remonstrate any further.

'Dear love, will you believe me when I tell you that I'm longing to take up my domestic responsibilities? I promise you I shall never want to leave you for any other reason than my work.'

'Pooh,' said Victoria, 'and I know what that will be—called out just as we're sitting down to dinner, home late, up early.' She smiled happily at him. 'I promise you, in my turn, I'll make you a splendid wife and I'll never grumble—well, almost never, if I don't see you to speak to for days on end.'

'Never that—I'm not quite like a GP, you know. I

seldom have to go out at night and once I'm home in the evenings, I expect to stay.'

They walked slowly round the little pond. 'When shall I see your house—you'll be working...'

'Tomorrow evening. I'll come for you and we'll go round it together and if there's anything you don't like or want altered we can see to it.'

'I don't think that's very likely. If it's like this house—it's quite beautiful.'

He looked pleased. 'Next weekend I'll drive you over to Loenen and show you the cottage. It's very small, but I think you'll like it too.'

'I looked at the map—there are some lakes near Wassenaar. Why don't you have a cottage by one of them?'

'The Loosdrecht lakes are larger—besides, I belong to the Royal Water Sports Club at Loenen. It's not far, you know—under forty miles and a fast run on the *autobaan*.' He looked at his watch. 'Time for lunch, my darling.' He kissed her swiftly, turned her round and walked her back to the house. 'Tell me,' he said, 'how do you feel about driving over here?'

'What—on the wrong side of the road? I'm not very good even in England.'

He laughed with gentle mockery. 'We'll have to alter that. When we're married I'll get you something small and not too fast, but you'll not drive alone until I'm quite sure you know what you're doing.'

They paused in the doorway. 'But I never know what I'm doing when I'm driving,' confessed Victoria.

The rest of the day was delightful and all too short. A leisurely tour of the house, with suitable intervals for talk, took up the afternoon while Mijnheer and Mevrouw van Schuylen rested in the sitting room. And after a cup of tea and wafer-thin biscuits which Victoria discovered was all there was to a Dutch tea-time, people called—

friends, a sprinkling of cousins and aunts and uncles and a handful of Alexander's colleagues.

They stood about the beautiful room talking to each other and to Victoria, switching from Dutch to English and back again with no apparent effort. Their lingual prowess filled her with envy and a determination to learn the language in the quickest possible time. And after the last caller had gone, they sat, the four of them, talking in the pleasant inconsequential way of a happy family, so that by the time they sat down to dinner that evening, Victoria felt that she had known her host and hostess for a great deal longer than a mere few hours.

Alexander left at ten o'clock. She had had very little opportunity of talking to him alone since the afternoon, it looked now, as he said goodnight to his parents, as if there would be no chance now. In this, however, she was mistaken. He crossed the room and pulled her to her feet, saying easily: 'Vicky darling, come and see me off,' and in the hall by the great door that was still standing open, he paused. 'You must be tired, my little love— all these strange people—but Mother and Father find you quite perfect, as I knew they would.' He held her close and kissed her gently. 'Sleep well, Vicky. Goodnight, my darling.'

Victoria watched him get into his car and drive away, and stayed in the doorway long after the sound of the engine had faded into the summer night. She longed to be with him and as she went back into the house she sighed a little, feeling lonely, and as though his mother had sensed it, she was invited to sit on the sofa and look through the family photograph albums. The sight of Alexander as a small boy, looking belligerently into the camera, somehow comforted her. 'He was a naughty little boy,' said his mother placidly, 'but never cruel or deceitful.' She turned blue, still beautiful eyes upon Victoria. 'He has a shocking bad temper,' she offered. 'Did you know?'

'Yes, I knew,' Victoria replied, 'but the only time I saw it, it was completely justified.' Jeremy Blake seemed very far away at that moment. She wasted no more thought on him but stated flatly: 'I've got a bad temper too. Not often, but I'm pigheaded.'

Mevrouw van Schuylen chuckled delightedly. 'Just what he needs,' she murmured, and closed the last album. 'Now you will like to go to bed, you have had a long day and everything is strange, is it not?'

In bed, very soon afterwards, Victoria sat against the big pillows, her arms round her knees. There was a lot to mull over and she wasn't in the least sleepy. Or so she thought; she had only just begun to think about Alexander when she fell asleep.

The next day, which she had secretly dreaded, proved to be delightful. She went shopping with Mevrouw van Schuylen after breakfast, driven into Leiden by the doctor, who dropped them off in the centre of the little city and went his way to deliver some lecture or other at the Medical School. He promised to pick them up later and take them home for lunch, for, as he darkly confided to Victoria, although his wife could drive, he didn't trust her an inch once she was behind the steering wheel.

They spent the afternoon in the garden and after tea Victoria repaired to her room to get ready for Alexander. She wasn't sure at what time he would come, but she was determined to be ready for him. She changed her cotton dress for a pink silk jersey of an exact shade to complement her hair, and put on her new coffee-coloured sandals, and because she didn't know how late they would return that evening, she put out a thin wool coat of the same colour. Her brilliant hair she had arranged in its three complicated loops, and her face, which needed little done to it anyway, was delicately lipsticked and powdered, with only the faintest hint of eyeshadow. She took a final look at herself, was lavish with Dioressence, and went downstairs just as the Mercedes drew up at the door. She was halfway across the hall when Alexander, coming in, saw her.

'I've waited all day,' he said, and kissed her so hard that she regretted the careful time spent on her mirror, for her make-up was a total loss.

They spent only the briefest of time with his parents; within ten minutes he had turned the car and started on the short drive back to Wassenaar. It looked a pleasant place, Victoria decided, as they reached its outskirts, with a feeling of spaciousness about it which she hadn't felt in the towns she had already seen. The houses stood in their own gardens, some of them quite large, and even the avenues of semi-detached houses looked secluded and well-to-do.

'Is this all there is of the town?' she asked. 'I haven't seen any shops.'

'There aren't many, and they're in the old village. It's a suburb of den Haag, remember, so everyone goes there to shop, except for local groceries and so on.' He swung the car into a short, secluded road with fields and trees on its one side and a scattering of houses on the other. Halfway down he edged the car through an open gateway and stopped before a low house with a thatched roof, so utterly unlike what Victoria had expected that she sat saying nothing, staring at it.

'Surprised? It's an old farmhouse—there are several around here. I've managed to keep most of it in its original form, though it has been added to here and there.'

She looked at him and said finally: 'It's not what I expected—it's heavenly. I can't wait to see inside. Is all this garden yours?'

'Yes.' He got out of the car and helped her out too and without letting go of her arm, drew her to the door. It was an old door of weathered oak and there was a bell pull beside it which Victoria longed to tug, but there was no need, for the door had already been opened by a short, round person, with hair screwed into a fierce bun, a cheerful face as round as herself and bright black eyes.

'Juffrouw Boot,' said Alexander, 'my housekeeper and treasure—I should die without her.' He smiled as he spoke and her beam became even more pronounced.

'Now then, Doctor,' said Juffrouw Boot, 'not to tease, I beg.'

She spoke English—peculiar English, but all the same, English. Victoria exclaimed delightedly over this fact and the housekeeper looked pleased and a little self-conscious. 'Not well,' she explained for Victoria's benefit, 'but necessary. Doctor has many English friends, I must understand for the easiness.'

Victoria, still a little at sea because of Juffrouw Boot's peculiar way of pronouncing, volunteered the opinion that that was a splendid idea and Juffrouw Boot, still smiling, ushered them in, closed the door behind them and retired to her kitchen.

The house was quite perfect, furnished with a care and taste and an eye to detail which caused Victoria to exclaim: 'Did you do all this yourself? The colours and the lampshades and the bowls of flowers and that sampler on the wall and...'

He knew what she meant and his smile mocked her a little.

'My sweet, what you really want to know is which women or woman had a hand in it, isn't that so? Several.' He had his back to her now, opening a window, but when he turned round again his mocking smile had gone. He was smiling but now with tenderness. 'Goose! Most of it I thought of for myself, when I needed help or advice I had my mother and my sisters and my sisters-in-law, all clamouring to assist me.' He came to stand in front of her and took her hands in his. 'Vicky, I've had girl-friends, but none so close that I would wish her to arrange my home for me. Only you, my future wife, will do that.'

'Oh, I'm so glad!' She searched his face. 'I'm a fool, aren't I? but I can't help wondering—any girl would—you must have been in love...' She paused. 'I'm not supposed to ask that, am I? but I can't help it.'

Alexander let her hands go and took her chin between a gentle thumb and finger and lifted her face to meet his eyes. They were very blue and clear and she thought she could see a gleam of laughter in them.

'I would be a shocking liar if I told you that you were the first woman I had ever fallen in love with, and yet in a way it would be true; I have imagined myself in love on numerous occasions, although perhaps ''in love'' is hardly the right term, but you are the first woman I have loved, my darling, and the last. Does that satisfy you?'

She nodded her head with its crown of brilliant hair. 'Yes, I'll not mention it again—ever,' she promised. 'You're not annoyed?'

'No,' he bent and kissed her lightly. 'I'm glad you brought the matter up, for I wish that there will be no secrets between us, my Vicky.' He slid an arm around her shoulders. 'Come and see the drawing room.'

She could find no fault with it despite the fact that very few of its furnishings were of the same period. The fireplace surround was square and solid and white marble, the wallpaper was of dark green striped paper which looked like silk, and when she studied it, Victoria dis-

covered that it was. The floor was carpeted in a peacock
blue which matched superbly with the walls and the
chair covers, which were cream chintz patterned boldly
with raspberry-coloured flowers and green leaves. There
were gilt-framed portraits on the walls—'Family,' explained the doctor when she stopped to examine them—
and the wall lights were brass with cream shades, only
the table lamps were raspberry pink, as were the cush-
ions on the sofa. There was a Regency worktable in one
corner decorated with pen-work and a painted firescreen
of carved pinewood stood before the empty hearth. The
further wall was taken up by a cabinet filled with silver
and glass, adding beauty to an already beautiful room.
Victoria stared around her, trying to realise that before
very long she would be sitting in that very room, with
Alexander on the opposite side of the hearth. She smiled
as she conjured up this domestic scene and her heartbeat
quickened at the thought of having him all to herself for
the rest of her life. For one awful moment she wanted
to burst into tears with sheer happiness; instead she observed:

'It's a heavenly room, Alexander dear. I wouldn't
want to alter a thing—it's perfect!'

The dining room was beautiful too. The table was of
a plain dark wood banded with holly wood and the
chairs grouped round it were simple and elegant; richly
cushioned in plum-coloured velvet. The sideboard,
which was vast, and a side table completed the furniture
in the room, but it was enough; its white walls, plum-
coloured curtains and many-coloured carpet gave it a
warmth of which Victoria thoroughly approved. She said
so with deep satisfaction as she was led across the hall
to a much smaller room—a sitting room, comfortable
and lived-in. Its furnishings of browns and tawny yel-

lows mixed nicely with the panelled walls and the elaborate plaster ceiling.

'This used to be the parlour of the farmhouse when it was in its original state,' Alexander explained. 'I use it for a sitting room and quite often have my meals here. My study's next door.' He flung open a door in one corner and showed her this rather austere apartment, lined with books, the round table in its centre weighed down with papers and a businesslike desk in one corner. Here, presumably, the doctor was in the habit of seeing such patients as came to the house; not too many, she hoped out loud.

'Very seldom—just occasionally it is more convenient. I much prefer to see them at the hospitals where I go or in my own rooms. Come upstairs, Vicky.'

There were more rooms than she had supposed, the largest of which was in the front of the house, which she viewed with a somewhat heightened colour, to the doctor's amusement. He lounged against one wall, looking blandly wicked while she strolled around, finding nothing to say.

'Well?' he asked at length.

'It's charming…'

'You like the colours? There's nothing you would like altered?'

She caught his eye and frowned because he was laughing at her. 'No—it's perfect. Why must you laugh? I've not done this before. I'm a little…'

He crossed the room in two strides and hugged her. 'Oh, darling girl, you look exactly as you used to on the ward when the Major wouldn't behave himself! Come and see the rest of the house.'

Which was just as charming—there were more bedrooms, bathrooms and two roomy apartments which she rightly supposed were destined to be the nurseries. As they went slowly down the staircase with its carved banisters, she reflected that the house was a gem. The man who owned it must be rich; something she had never bothered much about. She had always known that he was comfortably well-off, but that wasn't quite the same thing. She said half accusingly: 'You must be rich—I didn't know...'

'No, my love, I'm aware of that. It didn't seem important enough to tell you about.' His voice was placid, and she answered readily: 'No, of course it wasn't,' because of course he was right, she wouldn't have cared if he had been a struggling doctor at the bottom of the ladder instead of at the top. 'Shall we live here always?'

'Yes—that is until I inherit the house in Leiden.'

'Not for years and years,' she interposed warmly. 'I shall love living here, Alexander.'

They stood together in the hall and he kissed her slowly. 'The house has been waiting for you,' he said softly.

They went back to the little sitting room then and ate the dinner Juffrouw Boot had cooked for them, and Victoria, unaware of what she was eating, declared that it was the best meal she had tasted. Afterwards they sat talking, close together on one of the sofas in the drawing room, until it was dark and Alexander got to his feet reluctantly and said: 'I'll take you home.'

Victoria bade Juffrouw Boot a happy goodnight and followed him out to the car and was driven, much too quickly, back to his father's house. The evening had gone in a flash and when she asked him when she would see him again he replied: 'Not tomorrow, I'm afraid, Vicky dear. I've a meeting in the evening and my day is pretty well filled up.' He smiled regretfully. 'I'll telephone you.'

With that she had to be content, telling herself that if

she was to become a doctor's wife she might as well start straight away getting used to playing second fiddle to his work. He went into the house with her, but only for a few minutes; Victoria stood on the steps watching the tail lights of the Mercedes disappearing down the darkened road, reminding herself that even if he couldn't come tomorrow, there was always the day after. She went to bed at once, to lie awake and remember each detail of his home—her home too, she thought sleepily, and closed her eyes on the delightful thought.

Alexander came and went all that first week, sometimes for several hours, sometimes for the briefest of visits; and not every day either, but the week passed pleasantly enough. She accompanied her host and hostess wherever they happened to be going and there was no lack of visitors to the house as well, numerous invitations to drinks were pressed upon her too and it was to one such gathering that Alexander accompanied the three of them. The house they had been bidden to was in den Haag, a tall, narrow building with a high gabled roof and a magnificent interior. There were a great many people there and Victoria, caught up in a small group of people she had met the previous evening, looked round for Alexander. She saw him at last, at the other end of the room, talking to a young woman, a blonde with silvery hair and a lovely figure. She was an elegant creature and they weren't so far away that Victoria wasn't able to see that she had a hand on the doctor's arm. Victoria felt a faint pricking of jealousy stir deep inside her and then turned her back upon them. Common sense, of which she had plenty, told her that if she were to allow her feelings to get the better of her every time Alexander spoke to a pretty woman, life would become a tiresome business.

She caught Mevrouw van Schuylen's eye and smiled and presently went to join her.

Much later, when they were home again and Alexander had gone back to Wassenaar, as they sat around discussing the evening, she resisted the urge to ask who the girl was. Alexander hadn't mentioned her, nor had his father and mother, but then, Victoria reasoned, they hadn't spoken to her. Maybe they didn't know her, although she had seemed on friendly—very friendly— terms with Alexander. She decided to think no more about it but applied her mind to the knotty question as to whether Mevrouw van Schuylen should give a small dinner party in the very near future, or wait for a few weeks until the weather, already warm, should be pleasant enough to have all the doors open and drinks on the lawn beyond the house. After a gentle discussion it was decided to wait, and from the way her hostess eyed her, Victoria guessed that there was a second, more important reason for waiting—their engagement.

On Saturday they drove over to Loenen with a picnic box in the boot because it was such a glorious day. The cottage on the edge of the lake was small with a narrow, precipitous stair leading to a loft, and three small rooms on the ground floor; a tiny sitting room, furnished very simply, an even smaller kitchen, well equipped and a bedroom. There was a pocket handkerchief of a garden before its green-painted door and at the back the grass, ringed round with bright flower beds, sloped down to the water. They ate their lunch there, watching the boats on the lake and when they had finished Alexander asked: 'Shall we take the boat out?' He looked at her as she spoke and she saw the approval in his eyes of her neat slacks and cotton shirt.

'I'd love that,' and she got to her feet without further waste of time and followed him on to the little jetty where his dinghy, a smart little boat, was moored. The breeze was light for once, but sufficient to take them to the other side of the lake, where they tied up and lay in the sun, side by side, hardly speaking but supremely happy. Victoria was sorry when it was time for them to go, but the journey back would take longer, for they would have to tack a good deal, and if they were to carry out their plan to dine that evening in den Haag, they would have to start without delay.

Alexander dropped her off at his parents' house with the promise to return within the hour. As she went upstairs to change it struck her that he used his car in the same way as other men used their legs, and the ten miles or so trip to and from his father's house meant no more to him than walking from one street to the next. She reminded herself happily that once they were married, he wouldn't need to make the journey quite as often.

She chose a patterned silk dress in cream and coffee brown, with a tiny pattern whose tawny shade exactly matched her hair and eyes, and was rewarded by the look in his eyes when she went downstairs.

'I didn't know you were here,' she said, a little breathless at the sight of him. 'You've not been waiting?'

He kissed her and then stood back to admire her. 'You're worth waiting for, dear girl, and there's plenty of time. Come into the drawing room for a minute.'

There was no one there. She looked at him enquiringly as she walked past him into the centre of the room. 'Are we waiting for your mother and father?' she wanted to know.

'No, I want to give you something, and I want to do it here.' He had come to stand by her, now he took her hands in his, smiling down at her.

'This, my darling.' He dropped her right hand and put his own into his pocket and took it out again to show her what was there. A ring in the palm of his hand, a magnificent sapphire and diamond ring, flashing its fire at her so that she gasped at its beauty.

She raised her lovely eyes to his. 'It's beautiful, my dear! I don't feel good enough for it.'

His brows arched and an amused smile touched his lips. 'There is nothing in this world as beautiful or as good as you, my dear darling.' He slipped the ring on to her finger and she exclaimed in some surprise:

'But it fits!'

'Remember you were trying on those rings Mother was showing you the other day? I got the size from one of them and had this one altered.' He kissed the hand he was holding and asked: 'Had you not wondered why I had not given you a ring?'

She answered him truthfully. 'Yes, I did, but it didn't worry me. I wouldn't have minded not having one, I'm just as much yours…'

A remark which called forth an entirely satisfactory response from Alexander. Presently, disentangling herself from his arms, she said demurely: 'I wonder if I should do my hair again? It must be shockingly untidy.'

'No,' said the doctor decisively, 'it's exactly right. Come along.'

'Your parents?'

He gave a crack of laughter. 'My darling, no self-respecting parent would wish to intrude at this moment. They will be here when we get back.'

They dined at the Saur, upstairs in the restaurant which had a faintly Edwardian flavour about it and was therefore a little formal. Victoria, as excited and happy as any newly engaged girl could be, tried to behave as though it wasn't the most marvellous day of her life, only her sparkling eyes and the happy curve of her mouth gave her away. She had no idea what she ate, although she knew it was something delicious because Alexander had ordered with such care, but she did know that they were drinking champagne. He raised his glass to her across the table and she smiled widely back at him and asked: 'Will you tell me about my ring—it must be old.'

'Yes, it's been in the family for a hundred years or so,' his voice was faintly amused, 'but I'm not going to talk about a ring, my darling, that would be a great waste of time. There are other things…'

He talked about other things, and Victoria's cheeks became pinker and her eyes widened and twinkled and shone and her pretty mouth never ceased to smile. Presently he put out his hand and took hers in it and she let it lie there, forgetful of where they were, living in her own happy world.

They had finished their coffee and were talking idly when Victoria saw the blonde girl again. She was sitting with a man—a short, stout man, not young any more, and when Victoria's eyes met hers she saw that the girl had seen them and, what was more, intended coming to their table.

'I think there's someone you know coming over to see you,' she observed quietly. 'She was at the party the other evening.'

She had time to note the expression—or lack of it—on Alexander's face as he got to his feet, but she had no time to think about it, for the girl was standing beside her.

'Alexander!' Her voice was pleasant and to Victoria's annoyance she spoke in Dutch after that so that she was unable to understand a word of what she said, only she could hear the warmth and intimacy in her voice.

But the girl didn't get far. Alexander interrupted her

in a cool polite voice. 'How nice to see you, Nina. I don't think you have met my fiancée?' He looked quickly at Victoria and away again. 'Darling, this is Nina de Ruiter whom I have known for a number of years. Nina, this is Victoria Parsons, who is staying with my parents while we make arrangements for the wedding.'

Nina switched over to English with an ease which compelled Victoria's admiration and envy. 'Well, I must say you've succeeded in surprising us all at last, Alexander.' She smiled in a most friendly fashion at Victoria, who forced herself to smile back with a warmth she didn't in the least feel. The creature had no right to call Alexander darling—or had she? She remembered how she had watched them talking together; perhaps Nina was an old flame of his, although she was making no attempt to arouse his interest now. Victoria, a fair-minded girl, had to allow that. She peeped at Alexander, still standing, his face quite composed as he discussed the merits of the restaurant, and when he drew her into the conversation she responded readily, indeed, she was actually beginning to like Nina in a cautious way when the latter said:

'I must go back to my table,' she smiled at Victoria. 'I hope we shall see more of each other—perhaps we could meet one day and do some shopping or see some of the sights.'

'I should like that,' said Victoria, and meant it. Old flame or not, Nina had shown no indication of wanting to attract the doctor. She said goodbye warmly and when they were alone again told Alexander: 'She's nice. I should enjoy going out with her. How pleasant to make friends so quickly!'

He gave her a long considered look which puzzled her. 'Playing deep, Vicky?' he wanted to know in a silky voice she had never heard before.

'Deep?' she echoed. 'What do you mean? What have I said that's deep?'

He smiled suddenly and she could have sworn that he looked relieved. 'Forgive me, darling, I was mistaken. No, don't ask me about it. I'm sure you'll find time to go out with Nina—I believe she's got a job, though I'm not sure what she does exactly.' His voice still held that thread of silkiness and she was quick to hear it.

'You sound as though you don't want me to—I won't go out with her if you don't want me to, Alexander.'

Her heart beat a little faster at the gentleness of his smile. 'No, darling, you will go out with whom you please, only try and fit it in in such a way that it doesn't encroach on Mother's plans. She is already very fond of you, you know.'

Victoria knew a red herring when she heard it. She was wise enough to follow this one. 'Oh, how nice! I'm glad, because I like her very much too. And your father. I hope you'll be just like him when you grow older.'

The remark had the effect of making him laugh, and the atmosphere lightened considerably as she led their talk on to lighter subjects.

Back home again she thanked him for her lovely evening, promised to be ready for him in the morning when he came and was about to wish him goodnight when his mother asked in some surprise: 'But, Alexander, surely you're staying the night—your room's ready, as it always is?'

He turned a placid face to his mother and his voice was just as placid. 'I have to return to my rooms,' he explained easily. 'There are some papers I really should attend to before Monday and I prefer to get them done tonight.'

His mother said nothing to this and Victoria allowed none of her feelings to show as she lifted a serene face

for his kiss. There was something she didn't know about
or even understand, something to do with Nina. She had
no doubt that he wasn't going to den Haag at all, but
somewhere else to meet Nina. It was a pity, thought
Victoria, her face still composed and smiling, that she
felt quite unable to ask Alexander just what he was up
to—and ridiculous too, bearing in mind the fact that they
had, only a few hours earlier, promised to marry each
other.

CHAPTER EIGHT

DURING the next week or so Victoria found herself, almost against her will, liking Nina. They had met again on the Sunday evening, when friends had turned up unexpectedly at the house at Leiden, and she had been with them. It had seemed to Victoria at the time that neither her host nor her hostess were particularly pleased to see her, although they had greeted her pleasantly enough, and as for Alexander, he had glanced up when Nina entered the room and Victoria had seen that same look on his face—impatience? annoyance? It was hard to tell, for it was gone at once and there was nothing to read from his manner, which was casual and friendly and gave no clue as to his real feelings. He chatted casually with Nina and when they parted it was with that same casual air, nothing more. Victoria told herself she was being an imaginative fool and spent the rest of the evening being very gay, and managed, almost, to forget about Nina and Alexander, who, if he had anything on his mind, was concealing it so successfully that by the end of the evening, she was lulled into admitting that she was indeed an imaginative fool.

The next few days passed pleasantly, sightseeing with Alexander's parents and always returning in time to greet Alexander each evening, dine quietly at home and stroll in the garden, or put on her prettiest dress and go dancing in den Haag. It was halfway through the week before she saw Nina again, this time in Leiden, where Victoria was whiling away an hour strolling along Rapenburg while Mevrouw van Schuylen was at the hairdresser's. Nina greeted her with a friendliness she found hard to resist; within ten minutes they were seated outside one of the cafés, eating ices, while Nina talked gaily about her friends, her job and the holiday she was planning. But presently Victoria found herself answering questions about herself.

'How long have you known Alexander?' asked Nina lightly. 'Surely not before he went to England this year?'

'No—I met him in Guernsey—my home's there. And then we met again in London, at the hospital where I worked. He's an honorary consultant there—I expect you know that.'

Nina nodded. 'Clever man, isn't he?' she observed, 'always has been, but great fun too.' She gave Victoria a smiling look. 'I expect you've discovered that for yourself, though.' She looked at her watch. 'I must go—I'm supposed to be collecting samples of silk. My boss has the job of redecorating the drawing room of a filthily rich old lady who doesn't really know what she wants— just so long as it costs the earth.' She laughed as she got to her feet. 'We must see each other again, it's been fun.'

They parted on the friendliest of terms and Victoria, watching her hurry back towards the town's centre, was puzzled at the faint feeling deep inside her that despite her friendliness, Nina wasn't really a friend at all. She shrugged away the idea and went to fetch her hostess, telling herself that she was getting altogether too fanciful. But that evening, sitting beside Alexander in the car, driving to Noordwijk aan Zee to dance and dine there, she told him of the meeting and had been a little disturbed at the sternness of his mouth and the little frown between his eyes.

'I had no idea she was in Leiden,' he said rather shortly. 'I imagined she worked in den Haag. To tell you the truth, we haven't met for some time—I've rather lost touch.'

Victoria waited for him to tell her more—at last she was going to find out just how well he had known Nina. She was disappointed; he seemed to consider the subject closed, merely remarking that he was looking forward to their evening together. It was on their way home later that evening after a splendid dinner and hours of dancing, that she tried again.

'Would you rather that I wasn't friendly with Nina?' she asked.

It was too dark to see his expression, but she had no doubt that he was frowning even though his voice was mild enough.

'My dear love, you may make friends with whomever you choose—who am I to interfere? I hope you will have a great many friends before very long.'

Which wasn't a very satisfactory answer. She agreed with him and didn't pursue the subject, for it seemed to her that despite his pleasant tone, she was skating on thin ice. It was a pity that she was so curious by nature, for she would really know no peace until she knew what had been between Nina and the man beside her. She was aware that she could ask him and he would answer her truthfully, but then he might not like her for asking. On the whole, she thought it better to say nothing. It was quite another matter, of course, if she managed to find out something from Nina.

It was Saturday again, and this time Alexander arrived in the morning, declaring his intention of staying the night at his parents' house. They spent the day driving along the country roads, through Haarlem and Alkmaar and then across the great dyke cutting off the Ijsselmeer from the North Sea. They had their lunch in Bolsward, in the attractive restaurant of the Wijnberg Hotel, and then drove on through Franeker and Leeuwarden to Dokkum and then back along the coast, to have tea in a tiny village café before they raced over the nineteen miles of the Zeedijk again. Once on the mainland again, they drove at a more gentle speed, back to Leiden, through the lovely late afternoon, and that evening visited the theatre in den Haag—an Agatha Christie thriller which Victoria had already seen so that she wasn't overbothered by her lack of understanding of what was being said on the stage.

She amused herself picking out words here and there, for she had learnt a few since she had been in Holland, and was encouraged to find that the language no longer sounded like gibberish even though it still made little or no sense to her. Alexander had said that he would arrange for her to have lessons, but he had said nothing further and she hadn't liked to remind him; she was content to wait, and he was a very busy man. He had said nothing definite about their marriage either; she had thought when he had asked her to visit his people that his intention was for them to marry as soon as he could arrange his affairs and get a couple of weeks' holiday, but nothing more had been said and she stilled a slight unease by looking at the beautiful ring on her finger. Perhaps she was being too impatient. She smiled to herself and slipped a hand into his and felt his fingers close round in a most reassuring fashion.

On Sunday they spent the day driving once more, for Alexander had said that she must see as much of Holland as possible. Later, he had added, they would explore together with more leisure. This time he took her through Utrecht and Arnhem and then up to Appeldoorn and Zwolle, to the southern parts of Friesland. They had lunched at a village café off delicious coffee and long soft rolls stuffed with cheese, and had had their tea in a pretty restaurant deep in the woods of Oranjewoud.

'I'd like to stay out for dinner, Vicky,' explained Alexander, 'but Mother expects us back. Perhaps next week—I thought it would be nice if we went down to Tilburg to see my younger brother—they can't come up here very well, his wife is expecting a baby any day now, but I'd like you to meet them. We could stay the night. I believe Mother told you that I'm giving a dinner party in ten days' time—just the family; it will give you a chance to meet them all.'

Victoria agreed that it would be delightful in such a meek voice that he began to laugh and presently stopped the car to turn to her and say:

'You don't think it's delightful at all, do you, Vicky? Hordes of strangers you'll have to learn to know and like.' He put out an arm and drew her close and kissed her. 'I love this meekness,' he murmured. 'If only I thought our married life was to be ruled by this unexpected facet of your delightful nature...'

Victoria giggled. 'You'd hate it,' she began, then: 'Would you really like me better?' she asked. 'I could try...'

'Stay as you are, darling girl, impulsive and a little cross sometimes and so very uncertain.'

'Uncertain?' She was surprised now. 'Me?'

'Yes—as though you had never expected to be happy or remain so.' He kissed her again. 'You're happy now, aren't you?'

She stared up at him. 'Yes—perfectly happy, my dear.' And her words stifled the unbidden thought that she would be even happier if only she could bring herself to ask about Nina, but she knew she couldn't do that; it would have to remain an unsolved mystery; she would have to resign herself to never knowing.

She was wrong. The next day Alexander went to Brussels for some meeting or other and Mevrouw van Schuylen had a dental appointment in den Haag. Victoria accompanied her and elected to stroll round the shops in Noordeinde while she was waiting for her. It was while she was poking around Boucher's bookshop that she saw Nina. They met almost as old friends and Victoria, having discovered that she had a free morning, asked her to take coffee with her. 'You see,' she explained seriously, 'I'm not sure where to go and I'm terrified of finding myself somewhere where they won't understand me.'

Nina laughed. 'That's not likely to happen here,' she exclaimed. 'Every shop has someone in it who can speak English and certainly understands it. We'll go to Formosa—are you alone?'

Victoria explained. 'But Mevrouw van Schuylen will be at least another half an hour or so—I don't know what she's having done, but she told me to call for her at about twelve o'clock.'

She sat down opposite Nina and looked around her. 'This is pleasant—I like the Hague.'

Nina smiled. 'A good thing too, since you are to marry Alexander and live in or near it for the rest of your life. When are you to marry?'

'I don't know. We—we haven't had much time to make plans—Alexander is so busy, isn't he, and when we meet…I expect the wedding will be in St Peter Port. My family live there, you know.'

'You haven't a job any more?'

Victoria poured the coffee and handed her companion a cup. 'No—Alexander asked me to give it up when I came here.'

Nina made a little face. 'So he really means it,' she said softly. 'I thought, when I first met you, that it was just a flash in the pan affair—a bluff. I must confess I hoped it was. You see, Alexander and I were to have been married.'

Victoria put her cup down very carefully, so as not to spill it. She felt cold inside and her mouth felt curiously stiff. She said at last in a commendably calm voice: 'Oh? I didn't know. I'm sorry, Nina; it must be painful for you, seeing us…'

'Yes, and more so because it all began as a stupid joke.'

Victoria refilled their cups with a steady hand. She had wanted to discover what the mystery was; well, she was getting her wish and with a vengeance; she must make the best of it. She made her face look pleasantly enquiring. Nina's statement explained a number of things—Alexander's look when he had seen her, his parents' polite coolness towards her when she had called that evening, Alexander's apparent lack of interest when Victoria had mentioned her…

'We quarrelled,' Nina seemed anxious to tell her all about it. 'Alexander's got a terrible temper, you know, we had an appalling row in that sitting room of his in the farmhouse—and do you know what was the last thing he said to me?'

Victoria shook her head at this purely rhetorical question.

'He was on the point of leaving for Guernsey, to stay with those friends of his there. He said: "I'll marry the first pretty girl I see in Guernsey." I thought he was joking and then I saw that he was still furious.' Her blue eyes rested momentarily on the ring on Victoria's finger. 'I flung that ring at him before I left the house. Even though he was still angry I never really thought he meant it. It seems he did, and now I come to think of it, he prides himself on being a man of his word.'

'Why have you told me all this?' demanded Victoria.

She was a little pale, but her eyes were steady and so was her voice.

'I didn't mean to, you're so sweet and a little naïve, aren't you? You might get hurt, especially if you really love him.'

Victoria's eyes widened in indignant astonishment. 'What other reason could I have for marrying him?' she wanted to know.

'Some girls would marry him for his money—he's got plenty and don't tell me you don't know that. He's good-looking too and he's got a way with women—a decided catch. Not you,' she added earnestly, 'and that's why it might be disastrous...'

She picked up her handbag and gloves. 'I must go— I promised to lunch with a friend. If it were any other girl I should hate to leave, but you're sensible as well as sweet; you'll want to think about it, won't you?' She got up and held out a hand, which Victoria took, not wanting to. 'I'm sure to see you around. Holland's so small.'

Victoria sat very still, watching Nina make her way through the crowded café. In a detached way she noted what a good-looking girl Nina was, and very well dressed. Alexander liked women to be well dressed, he had told her only the other day, and added the satisfying rider that he considered her taste in clothes to be everything it should be. He had even teased her a little and asked if she was going to be an extravagant wife.

She felt tears prick her eyelids and hastily poured another cup of coffee so that she had something to do. The simple act steadied her; she drank the coffee, which was cold by now, paid the bill and made her way out of the café. As Nina had so sapiently remarked, she would need to think, but not here or now. Alexander was away, she would have almost two days in which to decide what to say to him when he returned. The idea that she might talk to his parents about it flashed through her mind, to be instantly discarded. Going behind his back was the last thing she intended to do. She would be sensible and not get worked up about it, then she would be able to talk it over calmly with him when she saw him again. Having made up her mind to this, she stepped out briskly in the direction of the dentist's house, happily unaware that her face was so white that several people turned to look at her as she passed, convinced that at any moment she would drop to the pavement. No such catastrophe arose, however; she was a strong, healthy girl, and although she had received a shock she had no intention of giving way under it. She found her way to the waiting room and sat down to wait for Mevrouw van Schuylen, and when one of the patients spoke to her in deeply sympathetic tones she smiled politely and shook her head, not knowing that he had, in fact, taken her white face to be indicative of severe toothache.

If her hostess noticed anything strange about the appearance of her guest she said nothing about it, contenting herself with one sharp glance before launching into an account of the horrors she had endured in the dentist's chair. 'Do you mind if we go straight home, Victoria?' she wanted to know. 'I've had a local anaesthetic and my mouth is still so numb I might have some difficulty with eating.'

Victoria agreed with secret relief. Her hostess would doubtless rest after lunch, leaving her free to sit in the garden or go for a walk. A walk, she decided, a long one. It would clear her brain the more easily to remember every word that Nina had said to her. She felt wretched, but she made an effort to be her usual cheerful self during their drive back and while they ate the light luncheon Bep, the daily cook, had prepared for them, and sure enough, when they had finished, Mevrouw van Schuylen retired to her room, murmuring that dear Victoria could doubtless amuse herself for an hour or so and that her husband would probably be in for tea anyway. Victoria assured her that she had plenty to do and would perhaps take a walk later on, and was thereupon cautioned to be careful not to go too far or get lost, otherwise Alexander would never forgive his mother for letting his *lieveling* out of her sight. Victoria responded suitably to this little joke, accompanied her hostess to the foot of the stairs and waited while she mounted them and then made her escape into the garden.

There was a rough track behind its hedge, it was used by horse riders, little boys on bicycles, dogs and courting couples, and at this time of the day would be quiet. She began to walk along it now, not caring where she went, and presently when she came to a little clearing, very warm and peaceful in the sunshine, she sat down on a convenient tree stump and had a good cry. It did her a great deal of good and after a little while she dried her eyes, tidied her hair as best she might and began to retrace her steps. Now she could think; the tears had washed away a large part of the rage and humiliation and fright she had been storing up since she had met Nina that morning. There had to be an explanation, of course; when Alexander returned the next day she would ask him about it in a calm and dignified manner and his answer would, she had no doubt, put an end to all her fears and fancies. She felt better once she had made up her mind how she would behave; she would have felt better still if she could have blotted out entirely all that Nina had told her.

She returned for tea and found Alexander's father had just come home and only too glad to have company. He had been at the local hospital, where he occasionally gave anaesthetics and he was delighted to have an appreciative audience to listen to his day's work. They were discussing the merits of modern anaesthesia when his wife came into the room and the talk, naturally enough, became centred on her visit to the dentist, but presently, as she was pouring tea, she turned to Victoria and asked, 'Do you feel better, Vicky? You were so pale this morning, should you rest a little more, do you think? We have taken you out a great deal and as far as I remember we have never once asked you if you wished to go.'

They all laughed and Victoria protested: 'But I've loved every minute, really I have,' then went on more slowly, as an idea entered her head: 'But I have got a shocking headache. Would you think me very rude if I didn't go with you this evening to Mevrouw Vinke's house? I shall be sorry not to go, but perhaps if I have an early night I might get rid of it.'

'A very good idea,' agreed her hostess kindly. 'You shall dine with us if you wish and then go straight to bed.' She got up and to Victoria's surprise bent down and kissed her on her cheek. 'Dear Victoria, how quickly we have come to love you!'

After they had gone she went and sat in the garden. It was quiet there and the flowers smelled sweet and after a short time its peace had an effect upon her muddled thoughts so that although she was unhappy she was no longer despairing. She went indoors slowly, pausing in the drawing room to look around her at its treasures and so into the hall. She was halfway across it when the front door opened and Alexander walked in.

She stared at him open-mouthed, her delight at seeing him warring with the unhappy thoughts chasing each other round her head.

He came straight to her and took her in his arms and

kissed her. 'I got away early,' he explained. 'I thought you would have gone with Mother and Father, but they told me to come on here—that you had a headache.' He held her a little away from him and looked searchingly into her face. 'You've been crying! What's the matter, my dear little love—you're not ill?'

'No,' said Victoria, thinking how much simpler it would be if she were. 'I had a headache...'

'And what else?' He was still smiling, but the smile had changed and his piercing eyes seemed to bore into her head and see the muddle there. She took her time in answering him. She could, of course, deny that there was anything wrong, but if she did, he would know and question her again and she might blurt everything out without thinking carefully first... She said now:

'I met Nina today—while your mother was at the dentist. I went to look at the shops and I saw her. We had coffee together, at a place called Formosa. I liked it there and the coffee was excellent.'

He loosed her and stood staring down at her face and she was miserably aware that despite her calm voice, her mouth was shaking. Alexander smiled a little and took her arm. 'Let's go into the sitting room,' he invited. 'There's something you want to tell me, isn't there?'

In the cheerful little room he offered her a chair, but she shook her head; she had a feeling it wasn't going to be that sort of conversation, conducted comfortably from two easy chairs. Instead she leaned over the back of a high-backed leather chair, clinging rather tightly to it with taut fingers.

'Now, my love,' said Alexander in the silky voice she had learned to be wary of, 'shall we come to the crux of the matter?'

'That is the crux, Alexander. I—I don't think I *am* your love.'

His raised eyebrows and the sudden arrogance of his look sent her hurrying on, too fast, so that she hadn't time to pick her words as carefully as she had meant to.

'We were talking—you know—' She gave him an imploring look and he murmured smoothly: 'Indeed I know. Do go on, Victoria.'

'Well, she told me that you and she had—had been going to marry, only you quarrelled and—and she gave you back her ring—this ring—' She held out her hand for him to see as though that would make everything clear, but beyond according it a casual glance, as though it were a thing of no importance, he made no sign. 'I thought,' Victoria went on, feeling as though she were making a speech in a nightmare, 'that is, I've tried hard to believe that she was making it all up—for a joke, you know, but...'

He said swiftly before she could finish: 'And you have decided that it wasn't?'

She twisted her hands tightly together, not looking at him. 'You see, Alexander, I saw you when she came over to our table at the restaurant—you looked...' She couldn't find the right word and left the sentence, perforce, in mid-air. 'She described it all so clearly—your house and the sitting room, and if you really said what she said you did, then I...'

'What did I say?' He was lounging against the wall, hands in pockets. She peered at him and found his calm face quite terrifying. He was furious, but her own temper was rising too.

'Did you tell her that you would marry the first pretty girl you met once you got to Guernsey?'

He took a long time to answer. She listened to her heart thudding in her chest, so loud that he must surely hear it. 'Did you?' she repeated, her voice too loud in the quiet room.

'What if I tell you that I did say that?'

'But you did say it? Just those words?' She heard the despair in her voice and hoped he hadn't noticed.

'Yes, I said that.' He took his hands from his pockets and came to stand close to her.

'No,' she said fiercely. 'I can guess the rest. You've been using me as a sort of—of...'

'Decoy?' he suggested helpfully.

'Decoy to get Nina back.' She swallowed her rage and choked on it at his laugh.

'My dear Victoria,' he began; she allowed him to get no further.

'You went to see her after we got back from the restaurant that night,' she accused him fiercely. 'You said you had to go back to work...'

His voice was ice. 'Who said that I had gone to see Nina?'

'No one—I just knew. Oh, it all fits in so well.'

'You believe that I did that? A few hours after I had given you your ring—that I lied?' He walked across the room and stood staring out of the window into the quiet night. 'You're being impetuous and highly imaginative, Vicky. I...' He was interrupted by the telephone and after a moment's hesitation he lifted it from its cradle and stood frowning as he listened. When he answered, Victoria, who had picked up a few words since she had arrived in Holland, gathered that he had to go somewhere in a hurry. She was right. He replaced the receiver without haste and said briskly: 'I have to go straight to the hospital—it's urgent.' He was already at the door. 'We will finish this—er—argument tomorrow, Victoria.' He had gone before she could reply to his brief goodnight.

She listened to his footsteps cross the hall, the banging of the front door and then the sound of the Mercedes tearing down the road. When she could no longer hear it she went and sat down, telling herself that she was quite calm and he had only said that because that was the silly sort of thing a man always said when he was getting the worst of an argument with a woman. She sat for a long time while the evening darkened, going over and over their conversation, unable to conceal, however hard she tried, the one glaring fact that Nina had spoken the truth about his saying that he would marry the first girl...and if she had been truthful about that, why should she lie about anything else? She stirred restlessly. There must be some reason, and Alexander had said he would explain, and if he didn't love Nina any more she supposed it didn't matter too much, only the hurt of not being told was almost more than she could bear. The telephone rang again and she rather doubtfully lifted the receiver. Jaap was probably about, somewhere in the kitchen probably, but it seemed silly to disturb him. 'Hullo?' she asked tentatively, and heard Nina's voice.

'Victoria? You're all right? Has Alexander gone?'

Victoria's hand shook a little on the receiver. 'He left here about an hour ago. I—I thought it was the hospital...it was you.'

Her mind was so full of the fact that he had lied to her again that she didn't notice the tiny pause before Nina replied. 'Yes—I daresay he's been held up somewhere.'

'Are you at the same party as Mevrouw van Schuylen?' asked Victoria.

The pause was longer this time and she noticed it and put it down to Nina's kindness in not wanting to hurt her feelings, although it seemed silly to bother about a few feelings after what she had done.

'No,' said Nina at length. 'I'm at my flat. Victoria, you're sure you're all right?'

'Well, of course I am. Actually I was on my way to bed when you telephoned.' Her voice, she was pleased to hear, sounded calm and casual.

'Then I won't keep you. We'll meet again, shall we? And you shall tell me...no, never mind. Sleep well.'

'And that's a silly thing to say,' said Victoria to herself, packing her case with a fine disregard for her clothes. She would have to leave her second case where it was; she really didn't care anyway. She shut the lid on to the hopeless jumble within, flung on her coat, rammed a hat on to her fiery head and went, quietly so as not to disturb Jaap, downstairs. In the little sitting room once more, thanking heaven that Alexander had taught her one or two useful phrases in his own language, she dialled the number of the taxi firm so fortuitously written in the telephone book. It was easier than she had thought it would be, for a cheerful voice at the other end answered her peculiar Dutch with a brisk, 'At once, madam' in tolerable English. All she had to do was to wait for the taxi to arrive, which it did in a very few minutes. She let herself out of the house, feeling as though she were going to her own execution. She had written a short note to Mevrouw van Schuylen, not attempting to explain why she was leaving but begging for her forgiveness, and beside it she had left an envelope for Alexander. It contained her ring and nothing else because she hadn't been able to make up her mind what to write to him. She got into the taxi and asked:

'Could you take me to the Hague station, please—I want to catch the boat train to the Hook.'

The driver looked surprised. 'It will cost many gulden, miss.' He named a sum and she nodded her head. She had plenty of money with her.

'That's all right. There's time, isn't there?'

He nodded. 'Sure, sure. I get you there.'

He was as good as his word. She was in plenty of time, the train didn't leave until almost half past ten. Victoria bought her ticket without difficulty and when the train arrived, got in.

At the Hook she had to get a ticket for the boat—something, she was told politely, she should have done earlier. Luckily, said the friendly clerk, there happened to be a cancellation if she didn't mind going second class.

It wasn't a very comfortable journey, for there was no berth for her, only a reclining chair in which she lay uneasily, surrounded by family parties on their way home from holiday or service in Germany. Despite their cheerful chatter she dozed, and presently, when they had settled too, she slept, to wake cramped and chilly in the early morning. She got up then, made shift to wash and do her hair and make up her face and when the ship docked, made her way through the Customs and on to the London train. Here she was lucky, for a friendly steward asked her if she wanted breakfast and found her a seat.

She hadn't thought that she was hungry, but when the food came she ate with some sort of appetite, so that by the time the train got in to Liverpool Street Station, she felt almost herself, which was a good thing, for if she had been feeling anything less she would have found it difficult to take a taxi straight to St Judd's, beg an interview with the Matron and ask to be taken back as a part-time staff nurse. Matron had been kind and most forbearing when it came to asking questions, and when Victoria asked if she might be engaged on a weekly basis, had replied that yes, she couldn't see why not, 'For I daresay,' she remarked calmly and with no signs of curiosity, 'you may wish to change your plans when you have had the time to decide what you wish to do.'

But her interview with Matron was easy compared with her meeting with her friends. They had appeared at first unbelieving, then curious, and then, finally, avid for information. She had stalled them off, that first day, with vague remarks about changing her mind, and they had seen her pale face and refrained from asking any more questions, trying to cheer her up by saying how glad they were to see her back again. As a special favour, she was to be allowed to sleep in the Home, even though she was only part-time, on the strict understanding that she should find somewhere of her own outside the hospital by the end of a month—an arrangement which suited her very well, for she would by that time have found another, permanent job, as far away from Holland as possible, she promised herself.

It was almost frightening how quickly she adjusted again to hospital life. The patients, those who remembered her, including the Major, accepted her return as nothing out of the way, merely remarking that she was back again, was she, to plague them with her pills and medicines. There was a new staff nurse who had taken her place, a girl she had known for some time and of the Old Crow's choosing; a rather serious girl, who didn't joke with the patients, and who, although kind, held a little aloof from their small griefs and joys. But she ran the ward well under Sister Crow's eye; Victoria had no doubt that she would make a fitting successor when the time came. That she resented Victoria's return was natural enough and a sufficient reason for Victoria to look for another job, but somehow in the first days of being back on the ward she was quite unable to put her mind to this. She had written to her mother, a bald letter stating that she had decided that she and Alexander didn't suit and that she had returned to St Judd's for the time being; further than that she had done nothing, only lie awake at night weaving impossible fairy stories in which Alexander appeared suddenly to whisk her away to live with him happily ever after—fantasies which in the cool light of early morning she knew to be absurd.

She had forgotten, of course, that she would have to meet Sir Keith again. He had looked mightily taken aback, although he had mercifully remained silent, which was more than she could say for Jeremy Blake, who had come upon her in the office on her first day back and asked so many questions that she turned upon him finally and told him to mind his own business and he had gone away, a mean little smile playing around his mouth.

It was halfway through the second week of her return when Nina made a surprising appearance at the Nurses' Home. Victoria had just come off duty and was sitting, in company with some of the other staff nurses, in the sitting room of the Home, rather listlessly drinking her tea while those of her friends who were free debated as to what to do with their evening. She was on the point of agreeing to go to the cinema with them when one of the maids put her head round the door with a declaration that there was a visitor for Staff Nurse Parsons. Victoria put her cup down very carefully because the wild surge of excitement which had torn through her like a great gust of wind threatened to make her hands unsteady. She got up slowly, remarking in a matter-of-fact voice, for the benefit of the curious faces around her, that it was probably Mrs Johnson, and walked out of the room.

Nina was standing in the hall. She had her back to Victoria, which was just as well because it gave Victoria time to wipe the disappointment from her face and substitute one of mild welcome—indeed, she had her features so well under control that she was able to produce a perfectly natural smile. 'Nina—what a surprise! This is the last place where I expected to see you. Are you in a hurry? Would you like some tea, or are you just passing through?'

Nina eyed her uncertainly. 'I'm here to see you. I'm going on to Brighton tomorrow. I've a friend there...'

Victoria dismissed the friend. 'Me?' she asked. 'What about?' She managed to smile again and this time it was a little easier. Provided she didn't allow herself to think and Nina didn't stay too long...

'Could we go somewhere? Your room, perhaps?' Nina looked around the hall, which at the best of times was hardly private.

'Yes, of course.' Victoria led the way upstairs and into her little room, rather bare because she hadn't bothered to unpack her small possessions. She offered Nina the chair and perched herself on the side of the bed.

'It's difficult,' began Nina in her prettily accented English, 'to know how to begin.' She cast an apologetic look at Victoria, who, not knowing how to help, said 'Oh?' in what she hoped was an encouraging voice while at the same time nerving herself for bad news. Probably Nina was going to tell her that she and Alexander were married. No, it couldn't be that, for she remembered how he had explained to her on one of their lighthearted expeditions together—how many lifetimes ago?—that no one could marry in Holland in less than two weeks. Perhaps he was here, in London with Nina. Victoria wet dry lips and forced them into a smile.

'That tale I told you, remember? That Alexander and I were to have been married. It wasn't true. We were good friends—oh, we liked each other all right, you know how it is, but it didn't last. He never once suggested...I've never even been to his house.'

Victoria found her voice, a little high and wobbly. 'But I don't understand—you said you had quarrelled with him in the sitting room…'

'I knew what it looked like—he'd talked about it.'

'But,' said Victoria, feeling her way and anxious to get away from a lot of unnecessary talk about the sitting room, 'you told me that he said that he would marry any pretty girl…'

'I know,' Nina sounded impatient. 'He did too, but not quite in the way I said. He was in a frightful temper and he only said it to let me see that I didn't matter at all, do you see?'

'No,' said Victoria, 'not really, but go on.'

Nina shrugged. 'But there is no more. I did it to spite him, I suppose—the way one does—I thought it would be fun to see him squirm. You see, I counted on you losing your temper about it—and you did, didn't you? You wouldn't wait to hear what he had to say. There was never anything, but he would be too proud and too angry to say so.'

'But he told me—I asked him if he'd said that…about marrying the first girl, and he said yes.'

'Of course—it was the truth, although perhaps a little twisted by me. If you had waited until the next day you would have discovered that.'

Victoria said stubbornly: 'You said that—when you telephoned, you remember—he was going to the Hague to see you.'

Nina gave a little laugh. 'I said you were naïve, didn't I? I didn't, not in actual words. I'd telephoned the people whose party you were supposed to be going to, I thought we could meet and I would explain that I had played the joke on you, and they told me to ring the van Schuylens' house. You jumped to the conclusion that Alexander had left you to visit me, didn't you—and I simply could not resist another little tease, so I let you believe it. He went to the hospital, he really did.'

She took a packet of cigarettes out of her handbag and offered Victoria one and when it was refused, lighted one for herself. 'I suppose I should be sorry,' she reflected.

Victoria couldn't reply, she was far too busy holding down the magnificent rage that boiled within her, for once she started to say all that she longed to say, there would be no holding her. After a long silence she managed: 'I suppose I have to thank you for coming. Does Alexander know that you're here?'

Nina eyed her with amusement. 'Good lord, no. I don't want my neck wrung. You can do what you like about it, but leave me out, thank you. I've other prospects—I'm going to be married myself, to a nice, cosy rich man who thinks I'm marvellous. Isn't that nice?'

'Very.' Victoria had her teeth firmly clenched on the words her tongue longed to utter. 'What about us—Alexander and me?'

Nina got up, threw her cigarette into the waste-paper basket and strolled to the door. 'That's up to you, isn't it? After all, if you're so keen on each other it won't make any difference in the long run, will it? Only take my advice and make the first move. Alexander can be pigheaded when he has a mind to—you know that, surely? I'll see you around some time.'

She opened the door, went through it without a backward glance and closed it gently after her, leaving Victoria sitting on the bed, speechless.

Her speech returned after a few moments, however. She held a long and loud conversation with herself which relieved her feelings considerably, as did a short and violent fit of weeping, so that presently, composed but red-eyed, she was able to write a letter to Alexander.

The spelling of it was erratic and the punctuation not all it should have been, but nonetheless it expressed in no uncertain manner the fact that she loved him very much. This sentiment took up most of the long letter, but there was enough about Nina to make it plain to him that it had all been a dreadful mistake and would he please write to her at once and say so too. She sealed it without reading it through and went downstairs with it. She would have to go to the post office down the street in order to catch the post that evening. She was crossing the front hall when she met Jeremy Blake, coming from the doctors' mess, on his way out. He held the door open for her and asked:

'Where are you off to in such a hurry, Staff?' and she, dimly aware that he sounded quite pleasant for once, said hastily: 'The post—I mustn't miss it.'

He held out a hand. 'I'm going there myself, I'll post it for you.'

'That's kind of you, thanks. You won't forget?'

'Hardly, since I've letters of my own and it's only a couple of minutes' walk.'

She watched him go briskly down the street in the direction of the post office. Alexander would get the letter in a day—two days at least. Perhaps he would telephone her. She wandered back to her room, deep in vague, hopeful dreams.

At the post office Jeremy Blake paused to read the address on Victoria's envelope. He posted his own letters and then deliberately put hers into his pocket.

Victoria almost counted the hours during the next few days, but when the fourth day came and went, and no letter from Alexander, she began to wilt a little. She had been buoyed up by the thought that even if he was still a little angry with her for not giving him a fair hearing, he would at least write and tell her so. She began to jump each time the telephone rang on the ward and invented any number of excuses which would take her past the pigeonholes where the staff letters were sorted. On the fifth day she wrote again, and unlucky chance so arranged it that Doctor Blake should come into the office just as she was stamping the envelope. She had picked it up immediately, but not before, without appearing to do so, he had seen the address. He gave no sign, however, merely saying: 'I thought Sister was on duty; I wanted to see her about transferring Mr Bates, but tomorrow will do as well.' He turned to go and at the door said carelessly: 'Do you want that letter to go? It'll just catch the post at the porter's lodge if I take it with me. I've got to go that way.'

She would have preferred to have taken it herself, but she couldn't very well leave the ward, and if he took it, Alexander would get it that much sooner. She gave it to him.

The following morning, Doctor Blake, using the porter's lodge telephone, watched the head porter sort the ward post. He was close to the pigeonholes, so it wasn't in the least difficult for him to see the letters in the staff section and the letter with the Dutch stamp was within inches of his hand. The porter's back was turned and there was no one else there; it only needed a few seconds to transfer the letter to his own pocket before finishing his call and strolling away down the corridor. Presently, in the seclusion of his own room, he burnt the letter, just as he had burned the two letters Victoria had given him.

Very slowly indeed the days dragged by and Victoria, a little paler and a little more silent each day, found them endless. It was exactly two weeks after writing her first letter that she made up her mind what to do and by the afternoon she had done it—given an understanding Matron her notice for the second time in as many months, broken the news to Sister Crow, booked a berth on the Harwich boat for that night, packed an overnight bag and gone on duty for the last time. It had been a little difficult, leaving at a moment's notice, as Matron had pointed out to her, but as it was quite obvious to that astute woman that Victoria intended to leave anyway, notice or no notice, she had stretched a point.

Victoria, looking like a ravishing beauty despite her white face, put on her new summer outfit, lime green and cream, her hair crowned by an eye-catching little hat to match, and marched through the front door of the hospital. She handed the case to the taxi driver and got in herself and a passing workman gave an appreciative whistle at the sight of her. She hoped with all her heart that Alexander, when he saw her in a few hours' time, would feel the same way.

CHAPTER NINE

VICTORIA got to the Hague well before ten o'clock. She had had an uneventful journey, lying sleepless in her cabin while she went over and over in her mind what she was going to say to Alexander. She had dressed early and had a cup of tea, and gone, like a nicely behaved automaton, off the ship, through Customs and into the train waiting at the station alongside the quay. The boat had been crowded with tourists and reunited families and when she got off the train at the Hague it was to find the station there crowded too. She had had to wait some time for a taxi, and when at last she got one, she climbed in thankfully, gave the address of Alexander's consulting rooms to the driver and sat back with a mixture of relief and fright reminiscent of a visit to the dentist.

In less than an hour—half an hour, she would be talking to him. She closed her eyes and tried to imagine what it would be like, but in this delectable pastime she was frustrated by the driver who said over his shoulder: 'You are English? I show you everything as we go.' Which he proceeded to do, shouting instructions as to where she should look next as he sped down Spui, crawled through the complicated traffic of the Hofweg and finally turned into Lange Vijverburg. Halfway down it he was forced to stop for the traffic lights—a chance, he called to her, to get a glimpse of the water to her right and would she kindly look out of her window? Victoria looked, but the view was blocked by the car beside them. The Mercedes—with Alexander at the wheel!

He was staring ahead, apparently in deep thought and at the sight of him, so unexpected and so close, her heart did a somersault and then raced on as though by doing so, it might help her to get to him quickly. Her voice, when she found it, came out as a small squeak but loud enough. At the sound of his name, he looked round, straight at her, and her shaking mouth, on the verge of a smile, froze, for he looked at her, after a split second of surprise, with no interest at all. Beyond the faint arch of his brows and the hardening of his already grim mouth she might just as well have not been there. She met his eyes, blue and hard, across the small space between them and swallowed panic from a very dry throat. Even as she whispered 'Alexander,' the lights had changed and the Mercedes shot ahead.

In a film, she supposed, she would have tapped the driver on his shoulder and ordered him to follow the car ahead of him, but the Mercedes had a turn of speed which allowed it to dart ahead even in congested, slow-moving traffic, and the cab she was in was an elderly Peugeot. Besides, what would be the point? If he didn't want to know her now, why should he at any other time? For the first time since she had started out on her journey, she wondered if perhaps there might have been some easier, more sensible way of meeting him again. But it was too late now, she was here, in den Haag, and here she would stay until she had seen him and at least tried to explain.

The driver turned left and slowed down to inspect the houses lining each side of the narrow, well-remembered road. 'It's halfway down,' said Victoria in a voice, which, despite her best efforts, trembled slightly.

There was no sign of the Mercedes when she got out. She paid the driver, who told her to enjoy herself while she was in the city, a sentiment which she heartily reciprocated, and went slowly up the steps leading to the big door guarding the various consulting rooms within.

His rooms were on the ground floor, she remembered, and easy enough to find. She opened the door with his name upon it and looked inside. If her memory served her right, it was the waiting room, with a desk in one corner. The desk was very tidy today, with papers neatly piled and an open typewriter, and behind it sat a young woman with a long face, an uncompromising hair-style and large melancholy eyes. But when she saw Victoria she smiled and she wasn't melancholy at all; her smile transformed her face with its charm and Victoria found herself walking eagerly towards her, sure that she would help.

'I'm looking for Doctor van Schuylen,' she began, then stopped, because this girl with the kind face might not understand English. She need not have worried on that score.

The smile widened. 'You are English? A patient who wishes to consult? The doctor is booked up for today—tomorrow too—he is a busy man. If you would tell me…perhaps I could help?'

'I'm not a patient,' said Victoria, unhappily aware that her haggard sleepless face hardly bore this statement out. 'I—I know Doctor van Schuylen. I—I wanted to see him. It's important. I wondered if you could fit me in somewhere—I can wait.'

The girl looked sympathetic. 'You are a friend—you did not telephone? He has a house at Wassenaar, it would perhaps be easier…' The sad eyes became all of a sudden very sharp. 'You are, I think, Miss Parsons.'

Victoria went a little nearer the desk. 'Yes. You know of me—did the doctor…?'

The girl shook her head. 'The doctor, no, but I hear things, though I do not speak of them, you understand?'

She smiled again. 'Sit down, Miss Parsons, and when the doctor comes, perhaps he will spare a minute.'

Victoria sat, a little way from the door so that as he came in he wouldn't see her immediately. She wasn't sure why she did this, she thought probably because she was feeling cowardly. He hadn't looked pleased to see her that morning, even allowing for shock; she hardly felt that he would welcome her with open arms. She blinked back tears, thinking how wonderful it would be to feel his arms around her once again, but that, she knew, would only happen after she had had a chance to talk to him.

He came five minutes later and by then there was someone else in the waiting room; an old lady, very thin and shaky, with a high, carrying voice and wearing what Victoria privately considered to be a vulgar display of diamonds. Alexander wished her good morning as he entered and when he saw Victoria he made a small movement and stopped dead on his way to his consulting room. For a moment she thought that he wasn't going to speak to her at all, but finally he said: 'Good morning, Victoria,' and crossed the room and disappeared, followed by the girl behind the desk. She came out a few minutes later, ushered the old lady in and then came over to Victoria.

'I am sorry,' she began kindly, 'but the doctor regrets that he has no time to see you, also he has appointments in the hospital after he has seen his patients. He feels that you waste your time.'

'What I do with my time,' said Victoria with asperity, 'is entirely my own affair. I shall sit here until you close, and tomorrow, too, if necessary.' She smiled at the girl. 'You won't mind if I sit here, will you? I'm doing no harm.'

It was awkward for the poor thing. Victoria had a

pang of sympathy for her, but if she went away, who knows, he might lock the door, and that would mean going to Wassenaar, and even then he might not be home or if he was, let her in. She settled down, as quiet as a mouse, leafing through a magazine which conveyed nothing to her, while one patient after the other came in, waited and in due course was ushered into the consulting room. It was two hours or so before the last person went in and another half an hour before he finally left and Alexander came out himself. He looked thunderous when he saw her, but she had prepared herself for that. But she hadn't prepared herself for, or expected, the gentleness with which he spoke to her.

'Victoria, it is useless for you to sit here. I am a busy man, and there is no use in stirring over dead ashes, is there?'

That should have been enough to have sent her on her way, back to England, convinced that he didn't love her any more, but something, a stubborn streak in her nature perhaps, kept her chained to the chair.

'You can't turn me out?' she wanted to know.

He laughed a little bitterly. 'I—turn you out? If you wish to sit here for reasons of your own, please feel free to do so. You will excuse me?'

He was gone, and Victoria ignored the cold emptiness inside her and smiled at the girl to let her see that she was quite happy. She asked:

'May I know your name?'

'Bep—Bep Fisscher. I am the doctor's receptionist and secretary. I have worked for him for five years. He is a very good boss.'

'I'm sure he is,' said Victoria warmly. 'Miss Fisscher, do you go out to lunch?'

'No, I have my *broodje* with me and coffee I make here. The doctor comes again this afternoon and dictates his letters and if he wishes he asks me to stay until he is finished.'

Victoria resolutely dismissed a picture of Alexander with his head bowed over his desk, working, and got up to take a few turns about the room. 'Good. You won't mind if I stay, then? You see, I think that when he has finished his day's work he might find time...'

'You will be hungry.'

'No, I'll be all right.' A lie if ever there was one; she would be famished. The things one did for love! 'But I'd be grateful for some coffee when you make it.'

The coffee was hot and warm and sweet and filled up her empty inside so that she felt more comfortable. And Bep was nice; they exchanged information about their families and Bep was in the middle of an enthralling escapade of her youngest, naughtiest brother when the telephone rang. After that she had to get on with her work again and Victoria was quietly doing nothing, and even dozed off for a while. The nap refreshed her and she tried to be practical. She would have to stay somewhere for the night and she would have to eat; but surely before then she would have managed to talk to Alexander.

She sat back with her eyes closed, more sure than ever now that she had been a fool to come. Girls didn't go rushing round after men who didn't love them any more—or perhaps he did? But if so, why had he made that beastly remark about dead ashes? She had almost made up her mind to leave and go back to England on the night boat and never think of him again, when he came back. He nodded briefly as he passed her and she caught a whiff of tobacco and after-shave lotion and forgot her resolution in a dream which was presently shattered by the entrance of a middle-aged man who spoke to her quite sharply and when she looked at him helplessly, said whatever it was all over again, rather more snappily.

'He only wants to know if you're ahead of him,' said Bep, soothing him. But the little interruption had put a stop to Victoria's dreams. The day was getting on; just supposing Alexander wouldn't let her talk to him? She opened her bag, found her purse and counted her money.

It was, unbelievably, six o'clock before the last patient went, and even then Bep disappeared into the consulting room with letters to sign. Victoria tidied her already tidy person, added a little more lipstick and waited. Presently the door opened and Bep came out with Alexander hard on her heels. It was now or never. Victoria got to her feet and he stopped in front of her.

'Have you somewhere to spend the night?' His voice was polite.

She shook her head. 'Alexander—' she began, but was blandly ignored.

'Bep, would you take a taxi and go with Miss Parsons to a hotel—let me see—the Central in Lange Poten is comfortable and only a stone's throw away. Take the taxi on home to make up for the delay.'

This high-handed arrangement goaded Victoria into quick action. She made for the door. 'Thank you,' she said with tremendous dignity, 'but I can find a hotel for myself.'

He had reached the door first. 'Please do as I say.' For a moment she thought that he was going to say more, but he didn't, only took possession of her overnight bag, a strategic move she hadn't foreseen, so that she was forced to wait meekly while Bep covered her typewriter, locked up and finally joined them. Outside Alexander hailed a passing taxi, saw them into it, said good evening with grave politeness and got into his own car. Victoria, sitting bolt upright beside Bep, didn't look at him.

The hotel was very close and, she realised with some unease, it looked expensive. She got out, refusing Bep's offer of help, and went inside. It was full of Americans—wealthy ones, judging from their appearance. Victoria sat down in the lounge and ordered coffee, and presently, when it came, went over to the reception desk to enquire about a room. It was, as she had so rightly guessed, wildly expensive. Alexander must have thought that she had brought her entire bank account with her, or, more likely, he hadn't thought about it at all; rich people, she had discovered, didn't think about money. She finished her coffee, paid for it and left. She walked for twenty minutes or more, looking at a number of hotels from the outside and finally decided on the Harrison in Spuistraat. It was simple inside, very clean and not expensive. She ate a good dinner and went thankfully to her room where she counted her money once more. She had her return ticket, of course, but very little besides, because, strangely enough, she hadn't thought that she would be staying in a hotel. She had imagined that Alexander would be so overjoyed to see her that he would have carried her off to his mother's house. She laughed hollowly about it as she undressed. Well, she could manage one more day, then she would have to go back. She had been a fool to come and everything that had happened to her had been her own fault. She got into bed and sobbed quietly until at last she fell asleep.

She made a good breakfast in the morning even though she wasn't hungry, because she wasn't sure about lunch, and upon reflection, she paid the bill—she could always go back there for another night if she could raise the money, or better still, find something cheaper, but even as she made her cheerful plans with a determination

the new day had brought with it, she knew in her heart
that if Alexander refused to see her today she would go
back. It wasn't a question of pride, she hadn't any left;
it was a question of knowing, at last, that he wasn't
going to forgive her for thinking that he had lied to her.
They would be finished—at least, he was. And she—she
hadn't got around to thinking about the future yet. Perhaps she would go home and after a while, start life
again. Another life, without Alexander.

Bep was already at her desk when Victoria arrived at
Alexander's rooms. She looked surprised and a little unhappy as she answered Victoria's good morning.

'He is coming, isn't he?' she asked.

Bep nodded, her eyes more melancholy than ever.
'Yes—he's due now. There are several patients, then
hospital. Patients again this afternoon. He works too
hard—he has no time for anything else, but you understand why, of course.'

Victoria found this puzzling. Why should she know
why, unless Bep meant that as a nurse she understood
how hard doctors worked? She was still considering this
when Alexander walked in and when he saw her, uttered
something explosive in his own language and then, in
English: 'Oh, Victoria!' He didn't sound angry, just ex-
asperated, and the face he turned to her was white and
weary, but he went on into the consulting room without
another word.

There were quite a lot of patients after the important-
looking man who went in first; a well-dressed woman
with a small boy, miserable with a never-ending cough,
an elderly man, very blue in the face, a young man with
dreadful spots, a small girl who cried all the time despite
her mother's efforts to stop her and finally, last of all, a
small shabby woman, clutching a doctor's letter. She had
a downtrodden air which stirred Victoria's pity and she

was glad to see that Bep treated her with exactly the same courtesy she had accorded the private patients and when she ushered her into Alexander's room, she gave her a comforting pat on the shoulder. And twenty minutes later, when he ushered her out again, Victoria's unhappy heart was warmed by the kindly courtesy with which he treated her. Watching him, it struck her how little she knew of his work. How many beds did he have in the hospitals, and how many hospitals? She suddenly wanted to know and was pulled up short when she remembered that probably she never would know now, for it was no longer, and perhaps never would be, any business of hers.

There was no one else in the room now, only Bep in her corner, typing and Alexander striding back from the door which he had gone to open for his shabby little patient. His glance flickered over Victoria.

'You'd better come in,' he said, and sighed, and she was so taken aback that she made no effort to get up but asked stupidly: 'Me?'

'You.' He held the door open for her, waved her into the chair opposite his desk and then sat down, saying mildly: 'I have ten minutes precisely. I hope you were comfortable in your hotel? I believe the food there is very good.'

'Is it? I daresay.' She choked on sudden wrath. 'I had a cup of coffee there and then went and found another hotel for the night. Have you any idea how much it costs to stay in a place like the Central?'

He looked taken aback. 'Well, yes, a rough idea.' His eyes narrowed. 'Never tell me you haven't any money, dear girl. You must allow me...'

'You dare—you just dare!' exclaimed Victoria instantly, tiredness, missed meals and misery taking over from the calm she had imposed upon herself. 'I'll—I'll throw it at you, and anything else I can lay my hands on!' She stared round the room, intent on putting her threat into force, unaware that her fine temper had rendered her even more eyecatching than usual.

An expression hard to read passed over the doctor's bland face. He eased himself more comfortably into his chair and studied her leisurely.

'Tell me,' he asked with interest, 'why haven't you any money?'

His calm voice did nothing to mend her temper; if anything, it made it even worse. 'If you must know,' she spoke through her splendid teeth, her lovely eyes flashing, 'I didn't expect to stay in a hotel.' She paused and then went on in a rush, for what could it matter now what she said to him? 'I expect you'll find this very amusing. I thought that you would be—that you would take me to stay at your mother's house.'

Not a muscle of his face moved, although she had the strong impression that he was hiding behind a mask of blandness. What was more, he had allowed his lids to drop over his eyes so that she couldn't see their expression any more. He stared at her for a long minute without replying and then switched on the intercom on his desk and spoke into it. When he had finished he sat back and said gently: 'Dear girl, I think that you and I should come to an understanding.'

She got to her feet, determined all at once to leave—a ridiculous action after she had come hundreds of miles to see him and had hung around for more than a day waiting for just such a chance as she now had. 'I'm not your dear girl,' her voice, taking things into its own hands, as it were, came out in a furious wail, 'and you'll never understand me!'

She made for the door and was frustrated before she was halfway there by the firm grip of his hand on her arm. When he spoke his voice was very quiet. 'No, I don't suppose I shall ever understand you, although I shall try my best, but this I do know, you are my dear girl—you always have been and you always will be.'

Victoria scarcely heard him, and in any case she was by now in no state to believe him. 'You won't forgive me ever, will you, because I thought you'd gone to see Nina instead of going to the hospital—and I should like to know what I was supposed to think when you were so—so cagey about her. Go away!' she invited him furiously. 'Go away and marry some girl or other. I was a fool to come, and I might have known when you didn't answer my letter...' She choked on a sob as his hand tightened painfully on her arm.

'What letter, Victoria?'

'The letter I wrote to you.' She stopped to hiccough while two tears rolled down her cheeks. 'After I met Nina in London and she told me about you and her—and why couldn't you have told me?' she wanted to know furiously, the words tumbling over each other now that they could at last be released. 'I thought...you let me believe...and all the while it didn't matter at all...not bothering so much as to tell me, and making me sit here for days on end while you stalk about like a bad-tempered tiger. I tried to tell you,' she hiccoughed again. 'It was a long letter,' she finished in a miserable voice. 'I'll never...'

He sounded as though he was laughing. 'Darling, my darling Victoria, you sound like a river in full flood. Hush a minute, my pretty. Did you post this letter?'

He had called her his darling—his pretty. She said, all at once meek, 'Yes, Alexander, of course I posted it,' and then as she remembered: 'No, I remember now, Jeremy Blake took it for me because he was going to the post office. He took the second one too.'

'And my letters, did you get those, my beautiful girl?'

She smiled at him from a tear-blotched face because she was beautiful. 'No,' she said finally.

'Who delivers your post?'

She explained about the pigeonholes.

'So anyone going there could take the letters?'

'Yes—I suppose so, but who would want to do that— not Jeremy Blake?'

'I think that he might have done so—after all, he had several scores to pay off, hadn't he? I telephoned too, and you were either not there or couldn't be found.'

'Oh, Alexander, if I'd known! I thought you never wanted to see me again.' She got no further, for his hold on her tightened as he bent to kiss her. He continued to kiss her for some time and only stopped when she said: 'Alexander, dear Alexander, I didn't mean it, saying that you'd gone to Nina's instead of the hospital—only I was jealous...'

'And I lost my temper, my darling—I could have explained about Nina in a few words, only I chose to deliberately misunderstand you. You will have to teach me to keep my temper, Vicky.'

'I don't intend to teach you anything.'

'Oh, yes, you will. You'll bully me and nag me, and I shall love it and be a model husband and an exemplary father.'

She had leaned her damp cheek against the fine wool of his jacket and her voice, a little muffled, was indignant. 'Hark at you—half an hour ago you wouldn't even look at me!'

He put a finger under her chin and lifted her face to his. 'My darling heart, I'll look my fill now.' He kissed her once more and went on: 'Do you want to hear about Nina? There's really nothing to tell, and there are other, more important things—this, for instance.' He kissed her again.

'She told me,' said Victoria, dismissing Nina for ever. 'What other important things?'

'Getting married, for a start. This time I shall marry you out of hand, dearest, then we can disagree in the comfortable knowledge that if you run away in a temper I can come after you and drag you back by your beautiful hair.'

She viewed this alarming aspect of her future with equanimity. 'I shan't run away,' she announced finally. Then she remembered something. 'What did you say over the intercom?'

'I told Bep to postpone my hospital round for half an hour. We should go now—you shall sit in the car, or visit the Directrice, she won't mind.'

'Are you very important, Alexander?'

'I suppose so, my darling.'

'And rich.'

'That too.'

'I'd marry you if you were poor.'

He smiled at her very tenderly. 'I know, my dearest love. Which reminds me—can you leave St Judd's as soon as possible?'

'I did—I gave in my notice, you see. I thought—I didn't know what to do, I just hoped… What would you have done if I hadn't come?'

He grinned suddenly. 'Which reminds me to cancel my flight to London this evening. You see, I was still angry and hurt, but I had to find you even if it was only to tell you that I loved you and then wring your neck.'

'Charming!' She flicked her eyelashes at him in a most beguiling fashion. 'I could have waited,' she mused. 'I need not have come,' she added naughtily. 'My journey was for nothing.'

'A point of view I will endeavour to alter.'

She smiled up at him. 'Start now,' commanded Victoria.

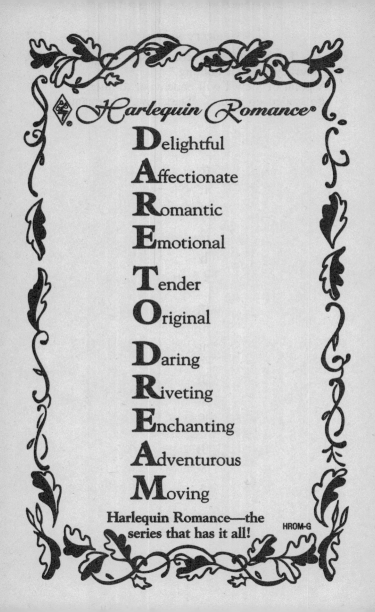

Harlequin Romance®

Delightful

Affectionate

Romantic

Emotional

Tender

Original

Daring

Riveting

Enchanting

Adventurous

Moving

Harlequin Romance—the
series that has it all!

HROM-G

HARLEQUIN ◆ PRESENTS®

HARLEQUIN PRESENTS
men you won't be able to resist
falling in love with...

HARLEQUIN PRESENTS
women who have feelings
just like your own...

HARLEQUIN PRESENTS
powerful passion in
exotic international settings...

HARLEQUIN PRESENTS
intense, dramatic stories that will keep you
turning to the very last page...

HARLEQUIN PRESENTS
The world's bestselling romance series!

Harlequin® Historical

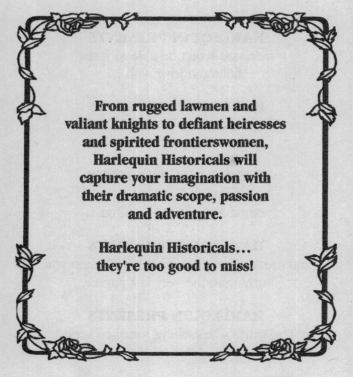

From rugged lawmen and
valiant knights to defiant heiresses
and spirited frontierswomen,
Harlequin Historicals will
capture your imagination with
their dramatic scope, passion
and adventure.

Harlequin Historicals...
they're too good to miss!